P9-CEV-728

# ENGLAND, FIRST & LAST

Also by Anthony Bailey

FICTION

Making Progress

The Mother Tongue

NONFICTION

The Inside Passage

Through the Great City

The Thousand Dollar Yacht

The Light in Holland

In the Village

A Concise History of the Low Countries

Rembrandt's House

Acts of Union

Along the Edge of the Forest

AUTOBIOGRAPHY

America, Lost & Found

Anthony Bailey

# ENGLAND, FIRST & LAST

Elisabeth Sifton Books
VIKING

ELISABETH SIFTON BOOKS • VIKING
Viking Penguin Inc., 40 West 23rd Street,
New York, New York 10010, U.S.A.
Penguin Books Ltd, Harmondsworth,
Middlesex, England
Penguin Books Australia Ltd, Ringwood,
Victoria, Australia
Penguin Books Canada Limited, 2801 John Street,
Markham, Ontario, Canada L3R 1B4
Penguin Books (N.Z.) Ltd, 182–190 Wairau Road,
Auckland 10, New Zealand



First published in 1985 by Viking Penguin Inc.
Published simultaneously in Canada

LIBRARY OF CONGRESS CATALOGING IN PUBLICATION DATA
Bailey, Anthony.
England, first & last.
Continues: America, lost & found.
"Elisabeth Sifton books."
1. Bailey, Anthony—Biography.
2. Authors, English—20th century—Biography. I. Title.
PR6052.A3184Z464 1985 942.1'2084'0924 [B] 85-633
ISBN 0-670-80404-5

Grateful acknowledgment is made to Macmillan Publishing Company, A. P. Watt Ltd., and Michael B. Yeats for permission to reprint lines from "Who Goes with Fergus," by W. B. Yeats, from *The Poems of W. B. Yeats*, edited by Richard J. Finneran (New York: Macmillan, 1983), and to Mrs. O. L. Spaeth for permission to reprint her letter.

Printed in the United States of America by
R. R. Donnelley & Sons Company, Harrisonburg, Virginia
Set in Linotron Baskerville

*TO BRIDGET*

ENGLAND,
FIRST &
LAST

# 1

On the train going south into England I slept against my mother's shoulder. Once I woke to hear the clickety-clack of the wheels and smell the chill sooty air, and as I saw where I was my thoughts tumbled in on one another: I was *back.* I was not in Dayton. I was going home. The woman who had met me as I got off the ship in Glasgow and whom I had recognized, after a moment's hesitation, as my mother, was here, sitting next to me in the first-class compartment, for the moment asleep, her cheeks damp with tears—tears of relief, of delight, of sadness, of all sorts of tangled-together emotions. My cheeks were wet, too; the tears had been contagious. Four years! The seven-year-old boy in gray shorts and blue gabardine raincoat to whom she had waved goodbye in September 1940 had become a youth of nearly twelve, wearing long trousers and speaking in a broad American accent. My suitcase was in the overhead rack, my twin-handled tartan-patterned holdall on the floor near the sliding door into the corridor. I could see my breath form clouds, and, shivering deeper into my overcoat, felt my mother move slightly. Her proximity was obviously natural and yet strange; I wasn't used to it. Although the rest of the unheated train was packed with people, servicemen and civilians on their way to London, we had this first-class compartment to ourselves, space and privacy bought at the expense of body warmth we might have shared in third-class. I was aware of something novel—that I was remembering things from before I had gone to America which I had until this moment forgotten, and was comparing them with things more recently got used to. The word rail*way;* the first and third classes; the sliding door with its pull-down blind. Small, framed, brownish photographs above the opposite seats displayed a Scottish hotel and a stretch of countryside in Derbyshire. The communication cord, in fact a short length of red-painted chain, hung in a recess over the other, outside door, to be pulled in an emergency, penalty for improper use £5. I had forgotten about pounds, shillings, and pence. Five pounds was a lot, the note itself a crisp white document with black copperplate script on it indicating the seriousness of promises made to the Bearer by the Bank of England. I remembered seeing a small stack of them in the bank my father had managed before the war. Thinking of money, I put my hand in my jacket pocket and felt the coin there, an American silver dollar, a keepsake and talisman, before I dozed off again.

The last few days at the end of the voyage had been exacting. An early November gale in the Irish Sea had forced our ship, an escort carrier named H.M.S. *Ranee,* to remain hove-to in the Firth of Clyde, waiting for the weather to moderate so that we could safely berth at Greenock. There had been farewell ceremonies with the officers, who had kept us busy on the ten-day voyage from Brooklyn. We were signed off as we had been signed on, a dozen privileged unofficial Boy Seamen, in effect passengers on what the U.S. Committee for the Care of European Children—which had handled my evacuation to and return from America—called quite rightly a Special Sailing. And then Glasgow, through which my mother and I had driven in a taxi, an Austin 16 saloon, perhaps large by British standards but which seemed about half the size of the Cadillac or the Buick or the La Salle that my Ohio foster family, the Spaeths, had had in the three-car garage alongside their Dayton home. Glasgow had been wet and gray, dark in mid-afternoon; there were gaps between houses, partly plugged with wooden scaffolding and buttresses, holding up what had been party walls and now showed the ghosts of staircases, with wallpaper and fireplaces as in giant dollhouses from which the floors had been removed. In the station buffet, with its blackout curtains pulled (though air raids in this November of 1944 were largely past—one reason it had been judged safe for me to come home), my mother bought cups of tea and cheese sandwiches; they tasted unlike anything I had eaten during the past four years.

"There won't be any food on the train," my mother said. Her tone of voice seemed to be preparing me for things that might take getting used to. But at that moment the general dilapidation and deprivation apparent to me—and perhaps all the more so because of what I would soon realize had been the fantastic comfort of my life in Ohio—were simply further aspects of my transatlantic adventure, which hadn't ended yet. I was more concerned about having been deprived of possessions I'd been forced to leave in Dayton, too heavy or bulky for my suitcase—a miniature printing press; a microscope Otto Spaeth had given me the previous Christmas; and my collection of war posters, now passed on to my Oakwood schoolfriend Fred Young. I was also excited at the chance to come back to a war I had been made to leave in the autumn of 1940—to come back to help finish off Hitler and his gang, to cheer on from closer range the Allied armies as they battled eastward across Europe to squeeze the German forces against the advancing Russians, and to experience—not to miss—some of the remaining dangers: V-1 flying bombs and V-2 rockets, the secret weapons Hitler hoped would swing the war back in his favor, were still falling in southeast England. My father was now part of this war effort, as

Americans called it; after a long wait for the bank to release him for call-up, he had eventually been commissioned in the Pioneer Corps, an unglamorous branch of the service that performed many dogsbody duties. He now had the interesting and—what was most important to my mother—relatively safe job of helping run a prisoner-of-war camp.

I dozed and several times woke up. An elderly railway guard came in and clipped our tickets. Traveling first-class, like taking the taxi in Glasgow, was an extravagance, I suspected—perhaps something my father had insisted on, for my mother's sake; perhaps an attempt to minimize for me any jolts of return. (Eloise Spaeth had brought me to New York from Dayton by train, traveling in a private roomette, which was certainly first-class though not called so.) Once I woke and found my left hand stuck in the narrow space between seat cushions and, as I slid it out, remembered how at the age of five or six I had found a ten-shilling note that way on the Isle of Wight train taking us to Sandown for our summer holidays. I wondered what sort of pocket money my parents could afford to give me, whether it would be the equivalent of the quarter a week I had got in Dayton, and what one could buy with it here. (The silver dollar in my pocket had been a Halloween concession from Orville Wright, the aged pioneer aviator, whom Fred Young and I had called on, trick-or-treating, the year before.)

I listened to the train wheels. The Spaeths had had a record on which an English Hollywood actor, Reginald Gardiner, pretended to be a train starting, stopping, passing over points and through stations. "Schenectady, Schenectady, Schenectady," went one refrain, the cleverly chosen name being that of a town which was an important junction for the New York Central railroad; we had passed through it on the way to New York. I wondered what sort of engine was hauling us south through England—I hadn't had a chance to see it on the station platform in Glasgow. London Midland Scottish, London Midland Scottish, went the wheels of our L.M.S. carriages. I remembered that off to the east ran the London North-Eastern, the L.N.E.R., and that we were heading in the direction of territories spanned by the Great Western Railway and the Southern, *my* railway, on which my father and I had traveled to London from Portsmouth when I set off for America. *I was on my way home.* The fact as an idea, a possibility, had been something that I hadn't let my mind settle on while I'd been in Ohio, though I had always known I was intended to stay with the Spaeths only "for the duration," however long that turned out to be. I had become almost a son to them, almost a brother to Tony Spaeth and his sisters Marna, Debbie, and Mimi. I was the Spaeths' English boy—a condition that involved being from England, that is, slightly different, but also involved being the Spaeths' charge, belonging to them in a way. I had ceded something of myself to them in return for the love and hospitality they had given me. I had passed successfully from E. Bennett Owen's sixth grade at Harman Avenue School. I had embarked on a promising career at Oakwood Junior High School—a larger institution, which seemed to hold before me all sorts of growing-up possibilities: the football squad; the track team; carrying heavier textbooks from class to class; having more to do with girls. And then Eloise had said, "Tony Bailey, you're going home."

My mother's arm was around my shoulders when I woke up on one occasion. I didn't look to see if she was awake. I didn't stir. Perhaps I recognized the four-year claim that—asleep or waking—she had upon me.

And on another occasion I thought that perhaps it was a dream, and I was still in my shared cabin on H.M.S.

*Ranee* and the carrier was lurching and rolling across the ocean, and the cabin door was opening. Someone, or part of someone, appeared briefly; then the door closed again. But it wasn't a dream. I felt my mother's arm. I saw the photograph of the hotel. I glanced at the door, and at the floor, where my holdall had been.

"The holdall's gone!"

It was out of surprise, first of all, that I cried out. But apart from a sweater and toilet stuff that I wouldn't have minded losing, the holdall contained presents from the Spaeths for my parents and my sister Bridget, and several books about airplanes and ships that were mine, and which I immediately wanted back.

For one so exhausted by events, my mother was quickly out into the corridor. In the next carriage she found the guard, returning from his ticket-collecting trip along the train. And in a few minutes he returned with a stern-faced sergeant who was already talking as he approached, apologizing for one of his men, who was going to catch it, truly catch it this time, bleeding well begging your pardon ma'am going to be for the flipping high jump since he was an idle no-good and this was the last straw. Unless my mother wanted to press charges, which she certainly had the right to, she could rest assured that the army would cope with the perpetrator of this petty criminal act.

All this while he was still cradling the holdall, the exhibit in the case, and I was wondering if I was going to get it back. The incident was disconcerting. For four years I had been in a part of the world where this sort of skulduggery had been uncommon or had not impinged on me. A British soldier, in khaki battledress! Didn't he know that I, too, was English, on his side? You could be robbed by your own fighting men.

"Oh, no—poor young man," my mother was saying. Apparently she could visualize the thief as a youth in need of care and better fortune. The sergeant, stern as ever, seemed satisfied by the generosity of this response—which the culprit did not at all deserve, mind you. "Thank you, ma'am," he said, handing over the holdall.

It was put up on the rack alongside the suitcase, the door was closed again, and my mother and I were left alone, sitting slightly apart as a result of the disturbance. The train ran on through the night, but for a little while it was hard to get back to sleep. The question that had been forming in confused fragments all round me since I landed from the *Ranee* was now abruptly shaped—what was it I had come back to?

# 2

EVERYTHING WAS SMALLER. IT WASN'T THE SUDDENLY reduced "standard of living" so much as it was that everything was closer, denser, more tangible. Like Gulliver in Lilliput, I found it hard not to bump into things. Only Bridget, my sister, was of course bigger than she had been, aged three, when I left, and was thrilled that I was back in time for her seventh birthday; her head was covered naturally in small, tight curls; my mother called her Tuppenny, a nickname whose monetary origin remained unexplained. Bridget walked with me around Edenholme, the bungalow my father had rented early in 1940 in order to move us further away from the obvious air-raid target of Portsmouth, with its naval dockyards. I imagined, but didn't say to her, that the whole house would have fitted into the Spaeth living room at 630 Runnymede Drive, in Dayton. As we made a tour, Bridget watched me touching things, objects I had forgotten and now remembered, and could almost have greeted with "Well, here we are again, you and I." Most of the furniture was coeval with the dawn of my memory—had been in the flat over the bank in Portchester and before that in Kingston Cross in Portsmouth, in the flat to which I had been carried a few days after being born, in a nursing home in Cumberland Road, Southsea, Portsmouth's somewhat select, seaside district. (That was in January of 1933, a year generally remembered for the rise of Hitler and the birth of the New Deal.) Some household items I had forgotten. I saw them as if for the first time while at nearly the same moment recollecting their existence.

Edenholme was a product of the sparse, symmetrical imagination of a local builder. It was built of orange-red brick, the material used in most of the other bungalows and semidetached cottages that lined Duncan Road. This rural thoroughfare in the hamlet of Park Gate was half a mile from the main road to Southampton; it twisted downhill past a timber yard that made punnets and baskets for the market gardeners and strawberry growers round about, and then ran alongside the yard of Swanwick station, a stop on the Portsmouth-Southampton railway line. At each end of Duncan Road were signs that said UNADOPTED, advertising—presumably for legal reasons—the act that Fareham District Council did not charge certain rates from property owners along it and therefore was not responsible for its haphazardly graveled surface, with ruts and potholes that held muddy pools of water after rain. From the road, several concrete steps led to a small white gate, set in a high hedge over which the roof of the bungalow could be seen—the gate bearing a board with incised letters, "Edenholme." The symmetry of the house was visible once one was through the gate, the front door smack in the middle between the windows of two equal-sized rooms, the bottom edge of the roof and gutter running immediately across windows and door giving the impression, as with a low forehead, of constrained development. The front door opened onto a narrow corridor: hemp doormat at one's feet; round brass casing of a clockwork-operated doorbell between the letter box and a frosted glass panel in the top fifth of the door that cast a pale light like that coming from the similar panel in an interior door at the other end of the corridor. Passing along it, I could almost touch the wall on each side by sticking my elbows out. A door on the left gave access to the drawing room. Facing it, a door on the right swung into my parents' bedroom.

Here the double bed with curved mahogany headboard and green eiderdown took up much of the space, the cramped residuum of floor occupied largely by a matching wardrobe and a dressing table, placed in front of the window, whose vertically hinged three-sectioned mirror reflected the room and its occupants but kept out a good deal of daylight. The drawing room was similarly filled by a suite of couch and two armchairs upholstered in floral-patterned fabric that seemed to make the already buoyant arms and backs swell even further, leaving the seats deep. Bridget bounced into one, rose briefly, and then sank, giggling. There was room between the couch and chairs for a round walnut coffee table and, along the walls, my mother's bureau-desk and a stand-up, windup gramophone. But there would have been no way of fitting in an upright piano, let alone one of the two grand pianos the Spaeths had (as if unable to make up their minds between a Steinway and a Baldwin) in the living room at 630. On the mantelpiece, over the small tiled fireplace, stood photographs of my father in uniform, of Bridget grinning, and of me, with a faint smile, in my American football gear.

The doorways to two small bedrooms, one Bridget's, one mine, faced each other next along the corridor. At the end of it, we came to the dining room, and from this, as one stood facing the garden at the back, the bathroom was to the right, the kitchen to the left. The toilet—the loo, no longer the john—was hard by the bathroom in a little chamber of its own, its flushing mechanism worked by a chain hanging from a high cistern. As I pulled it now, the cascading sound reminded me of the W.C. in the house of my mother's family, the Molonys, in Southampton, where the white toilet bowl showed a pattern of blue flowers and the maker's name for the model, surviving the spume and soaking of countless immersions, "Niagara." In the dining room I ran my fingers over the gray oak dining table, square and small for our contracted family, two extra leaves in their retracted place underneath. The sideboard was of the same oak. I had forgotten that its left-hand drawer had no handle—it had been broken long ago and never replaced. To prevent the drawer being pushed all the way in, and preserve a gap for fingers to grip its edge to pull it out, a green velvet-covered sausage-shaped cushion was left standing at the front of the drawer, its head poking out rather like a limp rag doll.

In the kitchen, with a small electric cooker, stone sink, and wooden draining board, the cream-painted cupboard had a central door that flapped down to form a work surface, disclosing within shelves and cubbyholes where various condiments were stored and a metal cone for holding flour was suspended, with a handle at its base that one turned to release the flour into a measuring cup. This reminded me of different aspects of "helping in the kitchen"—stirring puddings, shelling peas, licking out bowls in which the ingredients for cakes had been mixed—no doubt as much for the benefit it provided a mother keeping an eye on a child as for actual domestic assistance. A gas hot-water heater, which I had forgotten was called a geyser, hung up on the wall over the sink; a similar though larger geyser was in the bathroom, its pilot light always burning, the water-heating gas lighting with a *pop* when one turned on the tap, the water itself falling into the bath in a rather miserly stream. Unavoidable in America, hot water was, I realized—and without dismay—in short supply here in England. (Older evacuees returning may have found this more of a shock. One woman I know remembers coming back as an adolescent girl from Buenos Aires at this time and taking three hot showers a day; no one liked to tell her not to. When the hard facts of national privation got through to her, she felt pretty silly about it.)

Bridget led me to several outbuildings: first the small garage, semiburied in the slope of ground next to the road; it had held a Ford Popular saloon when I left in 1940 and was empty now. "Daddy sold the car when he went into the Army," Bridget said. I took in the fact that we were carless with no judgment attached—with no sense of "What a pity!" or "Gosh, and to think of all the cars the Spaeths had." It was simply a difference to be noted, part of the way things were in my new—or rather, resumed—life. We moved on to the garden shed, not far from the kitchen door, built of black, creosoted timber, the grain raised in corrugated ridges, leaving furrows where damp glistened. It contained my parents' bicycles, a lawnmower, a work bench, tools, pieces of timber, tins of paint, and my father's collection of nails, screws, cup hooks, and electric fittings, stored neatly in old jam jars. A shed like this went with just about every house to which, in the years to come, my parents moved. A tin opener was fixed just inside the door, my father for some reason having decided early on in married life that tin openers belonged not in the kitchen but in the shed, to which he carried cans of peas, beans, salmon, and sliced peaches for opening there, even if it meant a dash through the rain. In this Park Gate shed I eventually made a bookshelf to go over my bed, using a fine piece of oak, which looked good when varnished but took a long time to cut up with the one dull and rusty saw we had. Not far away was the air-raid shelter, rather like a concrete igloo grassed over, though inside it felt more like a tomb. I wasn't keen to go in again for the first time since September 1940, but thought I'd better show Bridget that I could put up for a minute with the damp, subterranean-smelling confines that she and my mother had endured for hours, day and night.

Then we ran down the garden. In Dayton, the large

house at 630 Runnymede had sat on a surprisingly paltry patch of ground, shaded at the rear by several tall maples that in the fall produced great piles of red-brown leaves. Here the proportions of house and garden were reversed. Immediately behind the house was a lawn on which in the summer of 1940 my father, home from work, had bowled tennis balls to me as I flourished my small-size cricket bat. There was a vegetable bed in which several rows of blue-green cabbages paraded. And then, sloping gently away with a tall untrimmed hedge on each side, the orchard: grass high and wet under forty fruit trees—the garden of Edenholme making up in bounty for the parsimony of the house. There were Victoria and damson plums, Conference and William pears, greengages and apples of many kinds—Cox's, Worcesters, Bromleys, Blenheims, Laxtons, and Russets among them. A few late ones were still on the trees, and a number of windfalls lay in the grass. Bridget had helped my mother wrap many of the apples in newspaper for keeping, in pieces economically torn from the thin, four-page editions of the *Daily Telegraph* or the Southampton evening paper, the *Southern Daily Echo,* then to be stored in cardboard boxes in the shed. They were apples that lacked the unblemished, standard good looks of Granny Smiths and Golden Delicious, the modern supermarket produce that in later years would cause my father to bemoan the shortage of what he called "good old English apples of the sort we had in Park Gate." They were frequently spotty, with gnarled skins or patchy color; they had flavors that, whether sharp or sweet, differed not only from tree to tree but often, so it seemed, from apple to apple on the same tree and were never, whatever the outside promised, disappointing.

Bridget showed me the place in the garden where, in May that year, she and my mother had been standing when a pair of twin-engined Messerschmitts had roared over low, guns firing—at *them,* she thought, as she and my mother dived into the grass. In fact, the German planes had been opening up on a line of Canadian tanks and military vehicles parked in a nearby lane, part of the forces assembling all over southern England for D-Day. Now, four months later, the fields stretched peacefully away beyond our orchard. I could see the railway line enter a short cutting on its way to Fareham: The barrage balloons that had hung in the 1940 summer sky over Portsmouth like fat fish had been lowered away. Perhaps at that moment I was taking in the wherewithal for thoughts that would later pop to the surface, such as that however dispiritingly broke and crowded Britain might come to be, its landscape made up for it. But I also found myself wishing that a lone Heinkel or Dornier would put in an appearance, to be chased and shot down by a Hawker Typhoon or Bristol Beaufighter.

Not only were the apples not the same as the American apples like Jonathans and Macintoshes (they were much better); different, too, for a four-year veteran of Spaeth cuisine, was much of the food put before me. Gone, thank goodness, were the highly touted (by Eloise) and dreaded (by me) asparagus, artichokes, and avocados—and summer squash, eggplant, and okra. But gone too were hamburgers and angel food cake and peppermint-stick ice cream. In those first few days my mother served dishes that had been my favorites, she said, "before you went to America." (This phrase, defining an apparently self-contained period of time, was used frequently in the years to come.) She made toad-in-the-hole (sausages baked in batter pudding) and spotted dick (steamed suet pudding with raisins). There were blackberry-and-apple pie and steak-and-kidney pie. I recognised as if it was an old toy or playmate the eggcup my mother put in the pie dish, inverted so that its base held up the center of the crust—which had a scroll decoration around the edge, made with a fork, and incisions in several places to let the steam escape. This eggcup was plain and white, goblet-shaped, but there were also eggcups with faces or flowers on them, and eggcups in the shape of chickens or Toby jugs. Boiled eggs in Ohio had been called "soft-boiled" and were served, decanted from their shells, in glasses, a process that made them seem insufficient. Now an egg once again might be the main course at tea, with toast or bread that my mother cut up for Bridget into thin fingers called soldiers, meant for dunking in the bright runny yolk. In Dayton, the day had slid through lunch and built to the crescendo of dinner, often a formal occasion in the Spaeth dining room. Here the day peaked at lunch, with a hot meal ("Your father always wants a hot meal at lunchtime"), and slowly declined past the way stations of tea and perhaps a snack for supper. Tea sometimes meant toast, especially on Sundays if a fire had been lit in the drawing-room grate, and if the coals were glowing sufficiently at teatime, bread would be impaled on the long, three-pronged brass toasting fork, and held before the fire. You had to be careful to keep shifting hands and changing the angle at which you held the fork, to avoid toasting your fingers, too. Bramble jelly was good on toast. (I had forgotten the Robertson's Golliwog label on the back of the jar.) I preferred it to the thin slices of brown bread and butter that my mother recommended I try with Shippam's Paste, a meat or fish spread that came in small glass jars with lids fastened by curious, circular metal straps—almost perverse in their built-in difficulty in use. A greater delight was in the rediscovery of Tate and Lyle's Golden Syrup, into which I plunged a spoon at breakfast, twirled it to collect as much as would stick to the spoon as possible, and then flipped in a gleaming parabola onto the porridge.

Many of the dishes my mother made then must have been created with difficulty: rations were small and getting smaller. One of the first things she did on my return was take me to a Ministry of Food office in Fareham to get me a child's blue ration book and allotment of clothing coupons. (Certain items, like bananas, were given out only to children—some returning evacuees may have had the impression that they were chiefly welcome for facilitating the purchase of such fruit, long hungered after by the adults to whom the children returned.) My mother talked of coupons and points; she managed cleverly with small amounts of lard and butter; she exchanged information with neighbors and fellow customers in shop queues about when and where scarce commodities would be available. She made jam and lemon marmalade and bottled fruit from the garden. She made summer pudding, the black, blue, and red fruit coloring the soaked bread in lovely mottled patterns. She made rabbit stew, and I felt fortunate if I had the piece with the shoulder bone, which with the meat removed looked like a sail. She made desserts that I connected with earliest childhood, like junket and blancmange, and she made custard with the yellow powder from tins labeled "Bird's" or "Foster Clark's." Another sort of yellow powder came in tins marked EGGS. My mother used this in recipes that in normal times would have required real eggs, and she sometimes cooked it with bacon or sausage as a stand-in for the genuine article, the mixture (powdered eggs plus water) forming a lumpy yellow splodge that gradually hardened into a sort of pancake. In fact my mother thrived on the difficulties of cooking in those years; later on, with a plenitude of raw materials in the shops, her culinary prowess found satisfaction in a simple, staple regimen of joints, chops, casseroles, and sausages ("excellently cooked," my father would say about the sausages, the slightly sardonic edge to the compliment evident, with much repetition, as a form of devotion). Any suggestion from Bridget or me that she might try spreading her wings would meet with remarks like "Oh, your father won't eat things like spaghetti"—or, for that matter, rice, macaroni, or noodles—and I would see that my father was gallantly refraining from saying that she never gave him the chance.

At Park Gate I was once again closer to what was going on in the kitchen than I had been in Dayton. In part this was simply because of the smallness of Edenholme—there was no butler's pantry between the dining room and kitchen—and also of course because there was no cook like Artie or butler like James, who had presided over their own domains at 630 Runnymede. Bridget and I assisted my mother. We carried things to and from the larder, a walk-in cupboard with an always open window, where meat and butter were kept under domed lids made of wire gauze. We set the table and helped wash and dry the dishes. The smell of cooking drew us to the kitchen; we weren't that far away. I was put to work stirring the gravy, seeing that it browned properly and thickened evenly: it was my job to see that there were no lumps in it. My mother at this point had been on her own with Bridget for three years, except when my father came home on leave. The sense of being needed—conveyed to me in the duty of gravy-making—may have helped reincorporate me into my own family, though an intermittent feeling of strangeness, of being on one side of a transparent but definite screen, through which I looked at them and they looked at me, took a long time to go away.

I got out my old toys. I put together the straight and curved sections of Hornby model-railway track, and, holding the driving wheels so that they didn't spin, wound up the motor of the bright green engine—the locomotive, I would have called it in America. Over the driving wheels on each side it had a small curved nameplate: *Caerphilly Castle.* After four years, it still worked. I watched it run around the track I had arranged on my bedroom floor, around and around, under the bed and out again. It wasn't much of a run compared with Otto's railroad system, allegedly built as a Christmas present for Tony Spaeth and me, which extended through three rooms in the basement at 630 and had quantities of rolling stock—freight wagons and passenger cars pulled by electric-powered locomotives in the colors of the Chesapeake & Ohio, New York Central, and Pennsylvania Railroads, and running past model towns and factories across real bridges and through tunnels in the walls. Caboose, I said to myself—funny word, nice sound. English trains had guard's vans, without the platforms at each end or the raised section of roof that allowed for windows giving a view forward over the train. Would I see a caboose again?

My Meccano set was still there, but I didn't take it out; it was pretty much like the Erector set Tony S. and I had had, and with which we'd made contraptions meant to be trucks and cranes. I turned to the African ceremonial paddles that Grandfather Molony had brought back from a tour of duty in the Gold Coast—called by my mother the white man's grave—at the turn of the century, and which were hanging on one of my bedroom walls. My grandfather had been a surveyor with the Ordnance Survey; my mother had brought him to Edenholme a day after a bomb demolished the house next door to his home in Southampton, and he had died a few days later of a stroke following the shock. The paddles were ebony; carved in an intricate pattern and pierced with holes, they looked like spears. I sat for a while on the edge of my bed pretending to be in a canoe on Torch Lake, in Michigan, where T.S. and I had gone to camp for two summers. Then I found my red Rexinecovered stamp album, and turned the pages—Bhopal, Bhor, Pitcairn Islands, Tahiti, Tchad, Togo. I had half a page of Maltese stamps, which had been sent to me in small batches by Grandfather Molony's sister, Great Aunt Bessie, who after nursing service on the Western Front in World War I became the matron of a military hospital in Malta. The king's head sat in one corner of the rectangular stamps, which featured Maltese scenes; the head of George V made one think of a sea captain, perhaps because of his beard, while that of the present king, George VI, beardless, even in miniature and profile seemed fragile. I had been told that George VI was a great stamp collector, and that he had a say in picking the designs of those stamps the British Post Office put out, saying no to those he didn't like. I had a lot of stamps that had never been stuck in, and, despite many rainy afternoons during the next few years, the quantity remaining in envelopes ever increased. It was a fussy process, licking the small opaque hinged mount that had to be stuck on the back of the stamp before pressing both stamp and mount to the page, hoping to get them straight.

The experience of having a bedroom to myself was unfamiliar—not sharing with Tony Spaeth any more, not being punished for talking after lights out (with him in one bunk bed, me in the other), not having someone to argue with, horse around with, and occasionally fight with. The three Spaeth girls had been at a remove from us—Mimi a baby when I arrived; Debbie a crucial year older; Marna, older still, away at school. Bridget, my close-at-hand but much younger sister, was clearly someone I had to look after and impress by example—someone, too, whom as I soon found I had the awesome power to tease. (A power I occasionally couldn't resist displaying. Bridget remembers that I handed her an apple once and watched her eat it, then said to her, "Did you like the taste of that worm?" She burst into tears.) Bridget had inherited some of my toys—my teddy bear, golliwog, and koala bear (sent from Australia by my mother's youngest brother, Vincent), whose back unzipped so that you could replace the battery that made its eyes light up. I was glad to see that I still had my white-hulled model yacht, named *Endeavour,* which I had sailed on the boating pond of Southsea common. It stood on top of my wardrobe, its sails in need of wind, reminding me of some of the first principles of full-scale sailing I'd learned on Torch Lake. Ready about. And mind the boom!

Before going to bed I looked at the Bulova watch Eloise had given me at the last minute as a farewell present. I didn't have to set it ahead an hour, as I'd had to some nights on the *Ranee.* I said my prayers, continuing to incorporate into them the Spaeths and my own family. (Please God, bring Daddy safely home from the war. Thank you for getting me home...) My mother said, "Perhaps tomorrow you'd better write to Uncle Otto and Aunt Eloise and tell them about your voyage back." Having spent four years writing home from America once a week, I apparently had a future in which I had to go on writing to America from here.

# 3

MUCH LATER, PEOPLE WOULD SAY, "IT MUST HAVE BEEN a dreadful shock for you, coming back," or, "Did you really want to come back?" or, "Wasn't it like being thrown out of paradise?"—the thrust of their remarks being that it was hard to see how, after life in all its richness at the Spaeths', I could easily have settled down in drab and battered Britain. I'm not sure. The transfer from the Eden of 630 Runnymede to Park Gate's Edenholme might look discomforting, even traumatic, but I don't remember conscious turmoil. At eleven going on twelve, most of one's concerns are immediate: e.g., what's going to happen today? Perhaps (I've thought since) the process of being evacuated, of leaving home and returning to it, made me notice things and observe differences. "That wasn't done that way in Dayton." I made comparisons. I asked why British houses didn't have storm windows. But at the time many of the unfamiliar aspects of life in England seemed like novelties—and I was a novelty, too, or at least unusual, an English lad who sounded like one of those G.I.s, who had spent four years in what most of our neighbors and friends considered an immensely exotic place. As I stood in the queue at the provisions counter in Peterkin's store, wearing my wooly camel-colored coat over a plaid lumberjack shirt, I heard my mother explaining my presence, and other women shoppers saying "Wasn't he lucky!" and "You must be glad to have him home." "Come back to help us polish off the Jerries, have you?" boomed Mr Peterkin, slicing off a fragment of cheddar with a wire cutter—though this note of welcome did not seem apparent in the grin on the face of the boy who delivered for the butcher, handing over a parcel of sausages at our door, as I said "Thanks a lot."

Even if there had been a need for contemplation, there wasn't much time for it. Swift decisions had to be taken about school. Many returning evacuees from better-off families were shunted off to boarding school at once, to schools for which their names may have been put down soon after birth, with money invested in special accounts and trusts to pay the fees. My parents couldn't have afforded to send me away to school even if they had wanted to. The autumn term was already two months old, and in my case it was an important one, since I was at the age when English children begin their secondary-school careers. In Dayton I had had four years of grade school and been furnished with a letter from Allan Zook, principal of Oakwood Junior High, saying that I had made a good start there and had "a fine attitude" toward my work. Armed with this, my mother took me to Fareham for an interview with the headmaster of Price's, a grammar school for boys, and for a test in writing and mathematics. Test and interview passed, the next step was a gents' outfitters in East Street. Here, in a small room at the back walled with white cardboard boxes, I was divested of my new world clothing and fitted into the uniform of an English schoolboy: gray blazer with a Price's badge showing a lion standing on its hind legs; gray shorts; long gray socks; gray shirt; striped red-and-gray tie; and peaked cap. Dayton had given me hope that as far as day-to-day clothing was concerned, my knees had disappeared forever. Here they were again. They stuck out like two red grinning faces between the bottom of the shorts and the tops of the socks—which had to be turned down neatly over the elastic garters meant to hold them in place. As for the flannel shirts, they were pulled on over one's head (the American-style coat-shirt, which buttoned all the way down the front, was only slowly making an appearance in Britain); they gave meaning to the phrase "hair shirt," when I later came upon it in Hendrik van Loon's *The Story of Tolerance,* which contained tales of the Inquisition and various martyrs to liberty. Comfort, clearly, was not a major element in my new life. At first the tie was a nuisance to deal with every morning, but as time passed it seemed to fall readily into the same somewhat shiny knot. The garters, which when new impressed a corrugated ridge on one's calves from the pattern of the socks, gradually lost their grip. In the course of the journey to school the socks crept down one's legs, undermining the effect of neatness and discipline the uniform was meant both to instill and to convey.

If there was any shock involved in coming back to England, turning up as a new boy at Price's brought it about. Price's followed the traditional public- and grammar-school practice of calling the lowest class or grade in the school the second form. There were two of these, 2a and 2b, the latter being regarded as more backward. I was put in 2b. The other members of the form had of course all been new boys together two months before; compared to me they were veterans. For several days I was the object of curiosity, disdain, and—with one or two lads—downright hostility. My American accent prompted feelings that I was overprivileged: a junior, civilian version of the U.S. soldiers who dispensed cigarettes and chewing gum and, no doubt helped by their higher pay, all too successfully romanced English girls. "Yank" was the obvious nickname for me, and "Yank" stuck, long after my nasal Ohio manner of talking had faded into a mere undertone modifying my basic British speech. "Yank!" —said with a taunt or ring of malice by a few in those days. "Yank!" yelled as a challenge by a fellow member of 2b, a freckled, pug-faced lad named Ginger, whose uniform already showed more than usual wear and tear because of playground fights in which he was generally the victor. Ginger's version of the war to date gave no credit at all to the Americans. In Dayton I had been compelled on several occasions to stand up for England but now I found myself forced into the role of spokesman for the United States—for generals MacArthur and Mark Clark, for PT boats and Mustang fighter planes, for Sherman tanks. This meant that during one midday break, at roughly the same time that Macauliffe's men were holding the German Ardennes counteroffensive at Bastogne, I was squaring off with Ginger in the playground. I attempted to keep him at a distance with my fists, but Ginger was more of a wrestler and came at me with arms extended, head lowered, ignoring my impeccable Georges Carpentier stance, and knocked me over. We were thrashing around on the gravel, egged on by Ginger's followers, when Ollie Johnston, the Latin and cricket master, stalked past on his way to inspect his precious cricket square, in which he took a year-round interest. We were hauled to our feet. Had it been summer, I later discovered, we would have had several hours of dandelion-weeding on the turf; as it was, we were told to report for Wednesday-afternoon detention in order to write out a hundred times each the cases of *mensa* and declensions of *amare*.

School was six days a week. On Wednesday and Saturday there were lessons in the morning and games in the afternoon. I reached Price's by train and foot—running down Duncan Road in the morning to Swanwick station, flashing my season ticket to the man on duty, charging up over the footbridge to the far platform, then climbing into a (preferably empty) compartment of the train, opening the window wide, and standing with my head half out of it in the wind as the train chugged through the Hampshire countryside—hedges, fields, copses, cows, a river—through tunnels, over and under bridges; then the junction with the Botley and Wickham lines, the Fareham West signal box, and into Fareham. It was seven minutes on the train, and a fifteen minutes' stroll or ten minutes' fast walk along West Street and up Trinity Street and Park Lane to where Price's sat on a hill on the north edge of town. I dashed past the house of Mr. Ashton, the headmaster, and generally encountered a few classmates for a game of conkers or marbles before the bell rang for morning prayers. (Conkers—I might have explained to my junior-high contemporaries—were the biggest and hardest chestnuts we could acquire by throwing sticks up into chestnut trees, with skewered holes through which a string could be threaded and knotted, and were matched in single combat as we took turns swinging at and hitting the opposing conker in the hope of shattering it. The marbles had to be bought in shops or won in the field of contest, and it was a sad thing to lose to an opponent a prized alley, tulip-streaked or veined like marble.)

The buildings at Price's were subecclesiastical in style. The assembly hall, which doubled as a gym, looked like a Victorian parish church in bright red brick rather than stone, with attached one-story wings containing classrooms. Behind these were several wooden huts in which physics and art were taught. One classroom, larger than the rest, was called the partition room; it was unpopular with the masters, who kicked on the wooden screen that divided it in two if they thought too much noise was coming from the other side. Most lessons took place in our own form rooms, where we sat at rows of wooden desks with lift-up lids and sliding metal tops over the inset inkwells. The tools of our trade were carried in rectangular wooden boxes, also with sliding tops: in these we kept pencils, penholders, nibs, and a rubber eraser, blue at one end for attempting to deal with ink smudges, white at the other for correcting pencil mistakes. Soon the middle finger on my right hand acquired a dent next to the top knuckle that was always ink-stained. In brown leather satchels we carried exercise books and battered textbooks, inside whose front covers our names were inscribed at the foot of lists of those who had been privileged to possess the books before us.

For four years my proper name had been Tony Bailey, spoken as if hyphenated, doubled up in that way to distinguish me from Tony Spaeth—though of course when we were separate (and we were in different grades at school) our friends called us simply Tony. Tony Spaeth and I used to refer to each other much of the time as T.S. and T.B. Here at Price's I was Yank to my contemporaries and to my teachers A.C. Bailey (for classroom purposes usually abbreviated to Bailey). The initials signaled the commencement of a usage that seemed part of a system fitting me back into English society, a usage that would follow me from school to the army, to university, into bank accounts, memberships, and subscriptions—and that I was never quite able to think of as me. I was also a little unsure about the Christian name Anthony, and still find it a touch pretentious, though I also find myself bristling a bit when I come across other writers of about my age with *my* name. In the early '30s, Anthony Eden was a handsome, suave M.P. active in foreign affairs, and it was perhaps his glamour, and the fact that Anthony was a good Catholic name, that recommended it to my mother. The middle C was for Cowper, my father's first name, which for a long time I believed he had been christened because of the poet

William Cowper; his middle name was Goldsmith, who was also a poet. But in fact the Goldsmith was simply a family name and the Cowper was in honour of Mr. Cowper, the veterinary surgeon in Shanklin, Isle of Wight, who successfully looked after the health of my grandfather's herd of dairy cows.

Ollie Johnston's method of teaching Latin was uninfluenced by St. Anthony or any other of the saints. A temptation to which he often gave way was that of physical violence, and in those first few weeks at Price's, as I tried to hasten across two months' untrodden ground, I was often the object of his quick temper, which permitted him to perceive only that the wrong case or declension had been sputtered forth by the boy who was reciting, and not that the boy had a good excuse for not being up with the rest of the class. Ollie Johnston looked like an American eagle, pouncing on his quivering victim with wild glare and outstretched talons. He would grab the short hair on one's temples, right next to the scalp, and pluck one to one's feet, there to stand reciting until the offending sentence was perfected. Latin meter remained a mystery to me; scansion was an obscure Morse code with strange signals called dactyls, spondees, and strophes (the hiatus, a pause for breath, was understandable); and finding the right occasion for the subjunctive or the ablative absolute was generally a matter of luck. But despite these handicaps I became good at Latin, and despite Ollie Johnston's punitive ways—which tended to produce a blur in my mind rather than linguistic clarity—I actually gained from his indoctrination a respect for Virgil, Livy, Caesar, and Cicero.

I had other problems apart from Latin. I had to get back into the habit of putting the *u* into words like *neighbour* and *rumour,* and writing aeroplane and sailing boat, instead of airplane and sailboat. Icebox and automobile had to be abandoned for an indefinite duration, and cans had to be tins. Relearning the intricacies of pounds, shillings, and pence and managing to multiply and divide them—why weren't they in neat, reasonable American decimals?—involved constant hazards and depressions. But *per ardua ad astra*—it was the RAF motto. In the report I received at the end of that first term I was twenty-seventh out of twenty-nine pupils in the form. The next term I was sixteenth. At the end of the summer term I was first—and was promoted into 3a instead of 3b. I wonder if I felt a need to come top to make up in some way to my parents for being deprived of me, or was the urge to succeed something that had rubbed off from the Spaeths?

In my mind now, Price's is not only an infrastructure of classrooms and lessons but an atmosphere, particularly of fragrances that seem to be on the very point of being breathed into my expectant nostrils. There was the slight smell of coal gas in the chemistry lab, presumably from the elderly rubber tubing leading to the bunsen burners. There was the sour smell of urine mixed with the sharper smell of disinfectant in the "bogs," the damp semioutdoor structure that housed the toilets. There was the smell of milk, often half-frozen in winter and on the verge of being "off" in summer, which we received in bottles of one third of a pint and drank while munching large, doughy currant buns, whose cost was a penny ha'penny (1½d). The milk was free, part of a government effort to raise the standard of health of British children that included bottles of cod-liver oil and concentrated orange juice distributed by the Ministry of Health to mothers of young children. And then in the school dining room there was the smell of gravy, partly covering slices of dark gray-brown meat, congealing pools that as in some geography-textbook illustration seemed to be seeping into lower strata through fissures in ancient rock.

In the playground Ginger swung a large red-brown conker that was as solid as rock and rival conkers (including mine) disintegrated from their strings.

# 4

THEN IT WAS COLD. WINTER—HITLER'S LAST ALLY—preoccupied Britain; in 1944–45 it was colder than it had been for fifty years. At Price's the classroom radiators were barely warm and the bunsen burners were kept alight in the chemistry lab. It was also wet. My dark blue gabardine raincoat was often soaked through by the time I got to school; my shoes dried on my feet, their brown leather streaked with white stains. Winter in Dayton had been as cold, if not colder, than this, but there we had had fur-lined leather helmets, earmuffs, and snowsuits—and effective central heating. Out of doors the fierce mid-continental cold had been dry, unlike this bone-piercing island damp. Indoors I had got used to the even seventy degrees of warmth brought about by the great furnace that James tended in the basement. In England, when the temperature went below what people regarded as usual, pipes froze; there were fuel shortages and power cuts; electric trains couldn't run (on the Fareham line we were still hauled to school by coal-burning engines). In Peterkin's queue, people wondered if Hitler had rearranged the Gulf Stream. At Edenholme we huddled close around the lumps of coal smoking in the drawing-room fireplace or sat over what was called an electric fire—a copper bowl, with wires glowing at the centre, which directed a narrow beam of heat toward certain areas of the body falling in its path, warming them slightly, while affecting the enveloping chill of the room hardly at all. Stone hot-water bottles, or rubber bottles in knitted woolen covers filled with near-boiling water from the kitchen kettle, provided the only salvation in bedrooms. I jumped into bed, slid shivering between frigid sheets, and attempted to get as much as possible of my feet and striped-pajama-clad legs around the hot-water bottle. By morning the bottle was cold and disagreeable to the touch. Frostbite might have produced injuries that would have let me feel I was emulating, on the daily trip to Fareham, the exploits of Scott and Shackleton; chilblains, the painful dark blue blisters that appeared on one's pink-gray fingers as a result of cold and ill-circulating blood, were badges without glory.

My mother said that bad luck came by threes, and as a long-range winter-weather forecaster she was spot on. The following winter of 1945–46 was also tough; the winter of '46–47 was catastrophic, and snow fell for the entire last week of January, burying the kingdom. There were fourteen-foot drifts in Essex; factories were closed all over the country and thousands of workers laid off; for three weeks no magazines could be printed (we didn't get our weekly *Picture Post* or *Radio Times*); electricity was cut off from nine to twelve and two to four each day; dog racing was canceled because no flood lights were permitted. Just as frozen pipes were followed by burst pipes, a second bout of blizzards and deep-freeze conditions in March was succeeded by severe floods. That third arctic winter in a row brought suggestions from the government that people should reduce the size of their fireplaces with loose bricks. Hugh Gaitskell, Minister of Fuel and Power, attempted to persuade us all to save fuel by not bathing often; he said, "Personally, I have never had a great many baths"—a statement I found sympathetic. Meanwhile our food rations got smaller. There was less meat in 1945 than in 1944; powdered eggs disappeared for a time early in 1946 until shipments from North America arrived. The Ministry of Food advertised such recipes as egg and onion flan, and sardine omelette, for which powdered eggs were suitable, *if* available. The ministry suggested putting nasturtium leaves in salad ("...with their hot taste, something like watercress...") and recommended exotic fish like South African Barracouta (as they spelled it), which they claimed could be made into scrumptious fish cakes and pies. Cans of a Norwegian fish called snoek were put on sale; tried by a few people, they were nationally condemned as a remedy too desperate to be eaten in circumstances short of starvation. (The ministry boosted both snoek and barracuda as being "low on points and price.") The Park Gate butcher's sausages, whose contents we didn't question, continued to be available, perhaps because it was uncertain whether for rationing purposes they should have been classed as meat or bread. Bread rationing was finally introduced in July 1946 and lasted for two years; the weekly ration was two large loaves for adults, one for children under six years of age. The so-called white bread was light gray, roughly the color of the paper in books then being published, on the reverse of whose title pages one read the imprimatur of the time, "Produced to authorized wartime economy standards." The word graffiti was still uncommon, though the practice of scribbling on walls was as always a way of venting frustration with the age. Mr. Chad was our symbol, a character simply created with crayon or chalk by drawing two semicircles and one straight line. The straight line was the top of a wall; one semicircle above the line was his head, peering over the wall; another reversed and much smaller semicircle was his nose, drooping under it. Beneath this melancholy figure was inscribed our message to whomever it might concern: "What, no chocolate!" or "Wot no beer."

In the *Daily Telegraph* each morning in my first winter back in England, I looked at the maps showing the advance of the Allies on the western borders of Germany. As I fought my way up through 2b, Montgomery, Dempsey, Bradley, Patton, and LeClerc, under Eisenhower's direction, pushed the German armies back toward the Rhine. In December 1944 it was judged safe to demobilize the Home Guard—in which my father had served before being called up—after four and a half years of guarding Britain against invasion. I was proud that my father was a captain, now looking after prisoners of war in Oxfordshire—and soon to take part in the bloodless liberation of the Channel Islands and guard German prisoners on Guernsey. (His letters and postcards were sent postage-free with the superscription "On Active Service," and were stamped by a censor.) In Park Gate we were already in a peaceful backwater: the great fleets of Lancasters and Flying Fortresses heading out to pulverize Hamburg, Dresden, and the Ruhr did not pass over us, and it was a rare misdirected flying bomb or rocket, at the end of its range, that came toward Portsmouth or Southampton. Clearly, as the singers on the BBC's Light Programme assured us, there were soon going to be bluebirds over the white cliffs of Dover and lilacs would again be gathered in the course of spring walks down English lanes. Yet there were intimations that, whenever the lights went on again, illuminating a world at peace, England wouldn't be quite the same as it had been before September 3, 1939.

Christmas in Edenholme, not quite seven weeks after my return, was, however, a return to the prewar custom of finding a pillow slip containing presents at the foot of my bed when I woke up on Christmas morning. In Dayton we had dashed downstairs to the living room to see what Santa Claus had brought, piled up in great mounds of splendidly wrapped packages under the Christmas tree—whose angel's halo brushed the ceiling. Here in Park Gate I looked down the bed and saw the pillowcase, which resembled a cloth draped over the barest remains of a meal; as I pulled it toward me, I realized that for what presents my mother had managed to get, the pillowcase was too big. Reaching inside, I found a pair of wool-lined leather gloves; a model-aeroplane kit; some hazelnuts; a bar of chocolate; and an orange. An orange—a present! My disappointment focused on it. I knew it represented everything that was in short supply—I liked oranges—and yet it seemed pathetic. I thought of all the oranges we'd had for the asking in Ohio, the quarts of orange juice!

But it was too cold to lie there. I heard my mother making up the fire in the drawing room, and took her the small bar of scented soap I'd bought as her present. A telegram from my father came during the morning, saying that he was thinking of us. After eating, we listened to the King's shy, halting voice on the wireless—the radio. Bridget had been given a play nurse's uniform, and I stretched out on the oval rug in front of the fireplace, pretending to be her patient, wondering what T.S. was doing at that moment. Bridget—to bring my attention back from four thousand miles away—showed me her appendectomy scar.

As a four-year-old in Portchester I'd had dreadful earaches, from which I'd wake at night screaming with the pain in my head. In the dreams I had then—or possibly they were a form of half-waking nightmare—the geometric-patterned frieze that ran around my room, topping the wallpaper, assumed a threatening life of its own, became a shape of oppression, constricting, tightening, moving in on me, quite real. I would sit up, yelling. The doctor had been consulted, a specialist looked me over. It was decided to carry out a combined tonsillectomy and mastoid-draining operation behind one ear. I kicked and screamed as the white-robed figures surrounded me and the ether mask was held firmly over my nose and mouth; when I woke up in the ward next morning it was clear to me that I would never talk again, though in a little while ice cream and a visit from the surgeon began to persuade me that things weren't quite as bad as I'd imagined.

The war for various reasons was good for British health—less sugar, less fat, perhaps; harder work, less sitting around; and also the appearance of new medicines like penicillin and sulfa drugs. In Dayton I had had whooping cough and measles and winter colds but had otherwise kept fit, cared for by the Spaeths as one of their own. For my age I was a solidly built small boy, a good runner, swimmer, and boxer. Now, back home, I began to grow gawky. Hands and wrists dangled out of the cuffs of my school jacket; my long trousers, a privilege of the third form, were never long enough. "Growing faster than his strength" was the way PT teachers put it, finding me more than averagely hopeless at vaulting over the horse or shinning up a rope. The numerous silver cups and trophies my father had won at county athletic meets sat gleaming in their mahogany corner cupboard along with only one of mine, a cup I'd won in Chatham, on Cape Cod, in the summer of 1941, for doing the fastest dog paddle at the Beach Club. It didn't look as if I was going to add any more to the collection. On the games field I tried to make up with enthusiasm what I lacked in ability with a soccer ball or hockey stick, making exhortatory noises from the left wing. It was decided that I had flat feet. My mother took me to a clinic in Fareham where a doctor pronounced the condition possible of remedy by exercise. Every morning and evening I had to flex my feet, lifting my heels from the ground so that I was supported on the ball of each foot, stretching the tendons in the back of the legs—fifty times. While I did this I sometimes thought about the Indian dances with a similar toe-and-heel motion that I'd helped perform at Harman Avenue Grade School and Camp Fairwood. I remembered raiding parties of Comanche and Sioux that I had led with my friends Fred Young and Harry Ebeling around the changing rooms of the abandoned swimming pool on Talbott Hill in Oakwood. At the age of twelve I began to have those strong yearnings for moments past which are subsumed under the neat label of nostalgia and which in after years occasionally became incapacitating, though I was never affected to the extent of some young British soldiers who served in North America during the Revolutionary War and who were said to have pined away there and died from *nostalgie.*

Our GP in Park Gate was an affable Scotsman who was a hero to my mother because he had rightly diagnosed Bridget's stomach pains a year before and got her smartly into Southampton hospital where her appendix was removed just before it burst. We were in the last year or so of a system whereby roughly 10 percent of the patients on what was called the doctor's panel received, after a means test, free treatment, while the rest paid whatever the doctor thought he should charge and they could afford—in our case a modest two shillings and sixpence for a surgery visit. One of the first features of the new welfare state, introduced in the early summer of 1945 by the Conservative caretaker administration—which governed for a few months between the resignation of the coalition National government and the election that produced a Labour government with a large majority—was the payment of family allowances directly to the mother of children. My mother received a small weekly sum for Bridget and me. The Education Act of 1944 had provided for compulsory free schooling for all children to the age of fifteen—and free beyond that for those who wanted to stay on in sixth forms and compete for county major scholarships to university. The National Health Service and National Insurance Scheme were to be inaugurated in 1948; the Health Service was resolutely but unsuccessfully opposed by the British Medical Association, many of whose members seemed to vent their grievance at "nationalized medicine" in the ensuing years by maintaining scarcely furnished, barely lit, and generally ill-heated waiting rooms. If nothing was wrong with you when you joined the other patients sitting there, shivering and sneezing, the chance was good that there would be by the time you left.

# 5

I HEARD FROM ELOISE SOON AFTER GETTING BACK. SHE wrote from the Madison Hotel in Manhattan, to which she had returned after taking me to Brooklyn to board the *Ranee.*

> My dear Tony,
>
> Now you are gone and I am back at the hotel alone. There were many things that I wanted to say at the last minute but when the time came—it just didn't seem to be the time.
>
> I do want you to know that we loved having you every minute that you were with us for all the four years—even when I had to tell you to WALK down stairs.
>
> Tony is going to miss you very much. Perhaps your Daddy and Mother will let you come back and spend some of your summers with us....
>
> I can't wait to hear all about your trip. Tell us all you can without giving away any military secrets. Love to all at home and remember
>
> Eloise

I wrote in reply telling her and Otto about my return. They both wrote back. Eloise told me how Otto had given Mimi, now five, her first spanking: "She was quite bland about it but he was considerably shaken." Otto, who didn't allude to this directly, but wrote, "Mimi is getting lovelier every day and also a little naughtier," enclosed two U.S. War Bonds I owned, bought with money I'd earned doing odd jobs. He said that he and Tony particularly missed me, but he was happy that I was home—"otherwise you would never realize what your family have sacrificed. I know it is going to be difficult for you and I also know that you are going to take it in your stride."

Probably most of the time I was doing just that. But now and then I got out the small collection of objects I'd brought back from Dayton, and my stride may have faltered. I looked at my Cub Scout badges and the certificate that said I was eligible to become a Tenderfoot Scout, and set out on the bed the awards I'd received at Camp Fairwood—cloth letter Fs won for prowess in archery or canoeing, meant for sewing on sweaters. I also had a round red and black felt badge from the National Rifle Association, Junior Division, as a "Pro-marksman," whatever that was. I reread the brochures for Otto's company, Dayton Tool & Engineering, which promised "Accurate Tools, Delivered on Time." I had kept a paper table mat from the restaurant at the Moraine Country Club, showing the layout of the golf course there. Otto had numbered the holes and put arrows showing the direction of play. I had a number of small white cards that I had printed on my miniature rotary press with the names and addresses of many of my school friends. I looked at a snapshot, taken a month or so before I left, of me, Debbie, Mimi, and Tony S.—staring intently, very Ottolike—on the front steps of 630 Runnymede. On the back of the photograph Debbie had written, "To our beloved 'Brother,' Tony Bailey." For some reason—perhaps the suggestion of departedness in the word beloved—this inscription made me think of the cards asking for prayers for the repose of a person's soul that one found sandwiched in the gold-edged pages of missals.

At Christmas and my birthday in early January, letters came from others. I heard from the Australian air-force officers serving at Wright Field who had been billeted in two of the Spaeths' attic bedrooms and whose shoes I had shined to make pocket money. Perhaps because I had been a reminder for them of the mother country or because, like me, they too had been far from home, they had treated me as a pal, albeit a junior one. Ron Wilson, a squadron leader, wrote to say he had been made a wing commander, that Tony S. had had a tooth pulled and had a face like a full moon next day, and that I was missed in Dayton. "However, you can't be in two places at the same time, can you?" Terry Bond, a flight lieutenant, wrote on the back of the same piece of foolscap to tell me things that the "Winker," as he called Ron Wilson, might have forgotten, such as the depth of the snow on Talbott Hill and the panic—except among the Australians, naturally—at the impending visit of an RAF air marshal to the Commonwealth mission in Dayton. He ended, "Keep that Bailey chin up at all times." The chin needed raising most on those occasions when I faced the dilemma of not being able to be in two places at the same time. T.S. wrote to thank me for a book I'd sent him and to tell me that he had got a BB gun—an air rifle—for Christmas, *and* a bike. The BB gun was something that I knew he'd wanted badly. (Perhaps anticipating jealousy, Eloise wrote in her next letter to say that the BB gun was a secondhand one that had been fixed up.) I continued to want a bike.

A few months later there was a sudden salvo of mail—twenty letters from my Junior High classmates, obviously under pressure of a teacher's assignment. "Everybody in our class is writing you a letter, or at least they are supposed to," wrote Russell Weller, giving the game away. The subject matter in each letter was largely the same. The track meet between Oakwood High and Wilbur Wright High, which Oakwood lost 49½ to 69½. The math work now being embarked on, which apparently caused some initial bafflement; my friend Bill Bettcher wrote, "In Arithmetic we are working equations. After we understand them we know how to work them." Bill modestly neglected to tell me that he had set the track record of 12.7 seconds in the 100 yard dash. Harry Schlafman told me that. Jim Schwinn described the effect on Dayton weather of a recent tidal wave in the Gulf of Mexico and added that he had got a 99 for a geography project about metal ores. Bob Neumeister made an effort to put himself in my shoes: "I imagine you found England a very different country than when you left it.... I imagine the welcome you received from your parents and sister." John Wood's mind was entirely on his pet racing pigeons. "I have four full grown ones and three squabs, which were hatched on Good Friday. I keep them in the attic." Dick Bigelow told me about the Seventh War Bond Drive. "Our class hasn't brought in too many sales but I hope we may pull up. The room which brings in the most bond sales gets an afternoon off. That's the way we are over here. We won't do anything unless there is a prize for first place." ("A" for perception, Bigelow!) My good friend Fred Young also told me about the track meet before demonstrating his burgeoning geopolitical sense, discussing the final phases of the war and the San Francisco conference to set up the United Nations organization. He added, "You'll be interested to know that Marilyn Sargent is getting along well. She is quite popular." (Marilyn, dark-haired and vivacious, had been in my sixth-grade class at Harman Avenue; I had been one of her many fans. No letter from Marilyn, or any of the other girls, however.) My other really good friend, Harry Ebeling, had already written to me twice, unprompted by teachers. (One letter was about FDR's death.) Harry had his own notepaper headed, "From the desk of Harry Ebeling." He decorated the margin of this letter with Allied flags—the Stars and Stripes, the Union Jack, the Hammer and

Sickle, and the Ebeling flag, a skull and crossbones he labelled the Jolly Hank ("Roger was drafted"). Harry also told me about the General Eisenhower Paper Drive, a nationwide effort. "All Boy Scouts collecting 1000 tons of paper are eligible for the General Eisenhower Medal. ... I am eligible for a medal and hope to get it soon." Harry went on, in his joshing way, "As you probably know I'm writing this letter from school. Most likely anything I tell you somebody else will say. (That last statement brings out the genius in me. What genius?) Will write soon (out of class), Eby."

Now and then in the years that followed I found myself wondering, What would I be like if I were now in America, growing up there, going to school with Harry and Fred? What would life be like if I had stayed in Dayton? These questions, pondered and almost wallowed in, made me feel a trifle guilty. Remaining in America—as some older evacuated children did, especially if their home circumstances had changed, through the loss of a parent, for example—would have meant casting loose irrevocably from my own family. How could I have done that?

# 6

I CAME BACK TO RELATIVES—TO MY MOTHER'S FAMILY, the Molonys, and my father's, the Baileys. Following the death of Granddad Molony, my grandmother moved back to their Victorian semidetached house at 5 Rose Road, Southampton, where the bomb damage had been repaired, and she was rejoined by my Aunt Connie (my mother's unmarried younger sister, a schoolteacher) and my cousin Patricia, a little older than me, whom Connie brought up after Patricia's mother died. Patricia's father—who had remarried—worked for Vickers Supermarine, the aircraft manufacturers, and had some glamour in my eyes as a result of having been part of the team that produced the Schneider Trophy–winning seaplane from which the Spitfire was developed. My mother's other and younger brother, who had emigrated to Australia, was serving in New Guinea as an officer in the Royal Australian Air Force.

Grandma Molony's family, the Breeds, had farmed on the borders of Cambridgeshire and Suffolk. Granddad had grown up in that part of the world; his father had had a pub and then a farm there. A generation before that, a Molony had come over from Ireland; before that, according to my mother, their ancestry could be traced back to Brian Boru, last of the Irish kings, who fell while defeating the Danes at Clontarf in 1014; I thereby joined the countless children of Irish descent who had been told they had a smidgen of royal blood. A more tangible connection was Great-Aunt Kitty, who made periodic trips from Connemara to England for the purpose (or so we gathered, when she called) of buying such things as a new alarm clock. "You can't boy a daycent alarm clock in Oireland," was her story. She also said her husband, Tom, had died of damp blankets while serving with the British Army in the First World War. The Molonys were proud of their connections with the Crown, but proud too of being partly Irish. (Later, my mother, only a quarter so, when she heard of some atrocity in Ulster, would say, "It makes me ashamed to be Irish.")

On the mantelpiece of the front room at 5 Rose Road sat the clock presented to my grandfather when he retired after a working life spent with the Ordnance Survey. There were always lots of maps at 5 Rose Road—printed on canvas-backed paper, folded and refolded into pocket-sized rectangles. I liked to follow footpaths on them, trace railways and canals, and try to work out from contours the steepness of hills. I admired the conventional signs: the crossed swords marking the site of a battle; the various graphic arrangements of tiny trees to indicate woods, orchards, or parkland and ornamental grounds.

My father's family hailed from the Isle of Wight, the flatfish-shaped island that sits three miles or so off the Hampshire coast. There we had gone for summer holidays before the war to stay in Sandown, the seaside resort where my father's parents lived in a house called "Netherwood"—semidetached, but grander and more spacious than 5 Rose Road. Grandpa Bailey had had a stroke in his early sixties and been forced to retire from his dairy business in Shanklin, a similar seaside town a few miles away along the island's southeast coast. He had been one of thirteen children—the only one, my father used to say, who had ever had a proper occupation. The others, including a large number of maiden aunts, managed to get by on the income left them by my great-grandfather, whose thriving island business empire included a haberdasher's shop in Shanklin, the first cinema on the island, and a considerable share in Shanklin pier. My father used to recall the big house his grandparents had lived in on the cliff path between Shanklin and Sandown—there was an "outlook" in the garden that provided a fine prospect of the Channel and the steamers and naval vessels taking the Spithead approaches to Portsmouth and Southampton.

My Bailey grandmother's family lived in Ryde, where the ferry from Portsmouth docked at the end of the long pier. Her father had a coal business in Ryde that was inherited by her brother, but according to my father, his uncle Fred never did a genuine day's work in his life. He played golf, was to be seen in the bars of Yelf's Hotel, and strolled around Ryde with a carnation in his buttonhole. I think my father sometimes regretted that he was part of the seemingly narrow branch of our Isle of Wight clan that took work seriously. Although he was no scholar and would have liked an open-air occupation like farming, he was firmly steered by my grandfather into a bank.

The prewar Portsmouth-Ryde ferries were paddle-wheelers—*Brading, Sandown, Portsdown,* and *Southsea*—operated by the Southern Railway. It was a thrill to get off the train at Portsmouth Harbour station, climb the gangway from the adjacent pierhead, and then hasten for a seat—depending on the weather—either in one of the saloons or out on deck. As the steamer prepared to get under way I would dash along a steel-floored passageway to a place where I could look down into the engine room and watch as the ship's telegraph rang and the huge light-green-painted arms and connecting rods began to move and rotate, amid jets of steam. Outside, water foamed from the paddlewheels. With its entire structure vibrating the ferry backed away from the pier for a few moments and then forged ahead, turning sharply out through the narrow, fortified entrance to Portsmouth harbor, where the hills of the Isle of Wight came into view. If the tide was high we cut across Horse Sand shoal and headed directly for Ryde pier; if not, a longer route was taken along Southsea beach, past one of Henry VIII's castles (built along the coast against the possibility of a French attack), past the boating pond where I had sailed my *Endeavour,* and past one of the round, forbidding, dark-gray forts that were stuck out in Spithead, part of a defensive system Palmerston's government had constructed, also against the French, in the 1850s.

On Ryde pier two trains were waiting. One was a set of light carriages used only for going up and down the length of the pier. The other was a more orthodox assembly of rolling stock, pulled by what looked like a small shunting engine, with a coal hopper attached directly behind the driver's cab; the cab had porthole windows at the back, overlooking the coal hopper, so that the engine could be driven just as easily in reverse on the trip back from Ventnor (where there was no turntable) at the far end of the line. In this train we went to Sandown. At Sandown there was also a pier—and though it didn't have a railway on it, it was, like most British piers, an expression of the last seaward thrust of the railway-building age which had created these tall, iron-legged structures decked with pine planks, from which anglers cast their lines while underneath the waves crashed and the spray flew up. In summer, steamers called at the pier to land or pick up day trippers. There was a theater where musical revues were performed, several restaurants and bars, and an amusement arcade among whose many slot machines I favored one, glass-cased, in which, for an inserted penny, one had the right for a short period to operate a crane with a grab in order to try and retrieve a small toy from an entangled heap of goodies before the coin-purchased time ran out. At the age of four I had won a prize on Sandown pier in a fancy-dress competition, dressed Tarzan-style in a fragment of imitation leopard-skin. Once I got lost on Sandown beach and had been found by my father near the pier, sitting in one of the skiffs that were rented out for rowing. Now, on the beach again, among concrete and wire anti-invasion impediments that hadn't yet been cleared away, Bridget and I swam and paddled. The temperature went up and down several degrees every time the sun went behind a cloud, and my mother would say, "Get dried quickly or you'll catch a chill." To her, a chill was somehow worse than a simple cold.

The Isle of Wight Baileys consisted most immediately of my grandmother who, widowed for some years, lived at Netherwood still, running the house with the help of a daily maid called May; my aunt Joyce, much younger than my father, who was on the point of marrying a merchant-navy officer, also an islander; and my father's younger brothers Jack and Jim, who, on the principle of First In, First Out, were demobilized before him. Jack, who loved horses, had served as a trooper in the Horse Artillery and proceeded to open a small livery stable on the outskirts of Ryde. Jim, who had served in the Royal Army Service Corps, most recently as port embarkation officer in Trieste, returned to run the haberdashery business, John Bailey's, expanding it from the store in Shanklin High Street to branches in Sandown, Cowes, and Ventnor. What I liked about Bailey's in Shanklin was the machinery used in paying for, say, the pair of socks being purchased for me. The money was handed over and wrapped in an invoice, placed in a cylindrical container, and whizzed to the cashier along overhead wires; then, after a pause for reckoning, the projectile containing the receipt and change came rocketing back.

Like many who are born islanders, my father both loved his insular home yet was glad to get off it. I wondered later whether he had ever surmounted the embarrassment he had felt at being made to carry some of his father's dairy milk to Ryde every morning on the train he took to school, to the amusement of his pals. In the postwar years he occasionally traveled to the Isle of Wight to take one of his elderly aunts out for the afternoon; they sometimes made him stop the car in what struck him as rather noticeable places in order to pick them a posy of flowers. According to my father, my grandfather had often rented a flat in Southsea, on the mainland, for the quiet winter months; when he took the family on holiday, it was generally to Brighton, on the Sussex coast. As they boarded the train at Portsmouth, Grandpa Bailey would tip the guard so that he would lock the carriage door from the outside and passengers at stations along the line would not be able to intrude into the Bailey compartment.

When my father was demobilized in the spring of 1946, he took us during his paid two months' demob leave for a week's holiday in Worthing, just to the west of Brighton. We stayed in a small, "private" hotel—the term "private" signifying that dining and drinking facilities were provided only for hotel residents. My mother—perhaps responding to her release from bearing alone the anxieties of house and children—succumbed to a severe attack of what my father called fibrositis, and stayed in bed for much of the week. My father, Bridget, and I sat on the chilly beach and watched RAF Gloster Meteors zoom past, practicing for a further advancement of the world air-speed record, 606 m.p.h., set by a Meteor the year before. The Meteor looked somewhat like the twin-engined, propeller-driven De Havilland Mosquito fighter-bomber, but was powered by Frank Whittle's jet engines, which took air in and blew it out.

I thought jets, apart from their speed, a bit boring; the Meteor compared with a Spitfire was like an electric train compared with one pulled by steam. My father recalled sitting with my mother on Ryde Beach in 1931, the year they were married, watching the Supermarine seaplane win the Schneider Trophy and the world speed record.

As families go, I was lucky with mine—though "lucky" was a word to which I developed a resistance. "Aren't you lucky!" my mother would frequently say in regard to achievements which, I felt, I had in fact worked hard for and which had little to do with fortune. But there was no doubt that I had been lucky in landing with the Spaeths in Dayton, and the thought sometimes occurred to me that I might have been born a Cambodian peasant, a Kalahari Bushman, or even *not born at all.* Providence had not done badly by me in the way of kin. The Molonys had a veneer of easygoing charm, under which lay a good deal of nervous, fussy concern, both for the way things looked and the way things might turn out. "Mind" was a word often on the lips of both my mother and her sister, Aunt Connie. "Mind you don't catch a chill not wearing a pullover." "Mind you don't trip over carrying that trunk downstairs." You were supposed to bear in mind—though in fact *they* were bearing in their minds—all sorts of hypothetical eventualities that might cause trouble; being carefree was being unprepared for the blows that fate had waiting on all sides, whether in the form of treacherous stairs or dangerous chills. There was therefore a regimen that had to be followed to get unscathed from one end of a Molony day to the other, including such obeisances to superstition or custom as not passing on the stairs (it was unlucky) and remembering to air the bed if one was sleeping in freshly laundered sheets (forfending calamity brought about by dampness—Great-Uncle Tom being a case in point).

Possibly because of all this anxiety close at hand, one of my father's favourite expressions was "Not to worry." Which isn't to say that *he* didn't worry, only that he was trying rather to encourage a congenial nonchalance that enabled life to go forward with less commotion and friction. Perhaps the Baileys did worry less than the Molonys, as on such subjects as whether doors and windows should be closed, preventing drafts, whether saucepans should be brought to the dining table, and what would be the right tea service to use if so-and-so called. Perhaps, too, it was my mother's "Molony-worrying" (as my father called it) that had looked ahead in early 1940 to the possible invasion of the British Isles by Hitler and foreseen a situation in which young Tony would be better off in the U.S.A. (Bridget, then aged three, was too young to be accepted by evacuation schemes for children unaccompanied by close relatives.) So although my father occasionally expressed concern as to what was going to happen to the nation with such-and-such a politician in charge or whether there would be another war if the Russians kept acting the way they did, he would generally bring to a halt his expressions of unease with the statements "Yes, it's all very worrying," accompanied by a laugh that was meant to suggest that, really, he was confident life was going to go on quite contentedly nevertheless.

Certainly the Baileys did not look like troubled people. They tended to have expansive, large-featured faces, of the sort found in portraits by Reynolds and Romney—prominent noses, big ears, ruddy cheeks; and they had a basic stratum of cheerfulness. My mother would return with Bridget and me from Sunday Mass, at which she would have prayed for a large number of individuals and causes, and my father would come in from the garden where he'd been pruning fruit trees and exclaim, with a big smile, "I hope you said one for me"—the implication being less that he didn't believe in the efficacy of prayer than that he didn't believe he needed it. One could get by, muddle through, without divine intervention.

In both families there were one or two black sheep, but for the most part Baileys and Molonys hewed to the middle ground of morality and moderation. I felt I was fortunate to be one of them, and lucky in that they encouraged me to believe that, in having spent most of the war in America, I had been given an exceptional opportunity to see beyond family confines. In a way this confidence helped sustain for a long time my suspicion that I was very different from my contemporaries, a feeling that all youngsters no doubt have about themselves at one point or other, but one that I regarded in my own case as particularly correct.

# 7

THE WAR ENDED IN ONE PLACE AND THEN ANOTHER. As the dust of battle cleared in Berlin, a blinding light flashed twice in Japan; it was as if the force that lay behind the world had been tapped. Once the sounds of celebrations died away, victory was soon viewed a trifle skeptically. Some demobilized British servicemen were said to be having trouble settling down in "civvy street." It wasn't long before suggestions were being made that we the victors should take pity on the Germans and send them used clothes and food parcels.

When nearly everyone else seemed to have left the forces, my father was demobilized. Later he told me that he had thought of staying on in the army; he had had "a good war," had neither been shot at nor had to shoot in earnest; his colonel admired his administrative abilities and he had ended his military career as adjutant of his unit; he was popular with many of the prisoners in the camp he helped to run—one, an artist, made several drawings for him; two or three for a while corresponded with him. But the army was offering only short-service commissions, which didn't give security of employment beyond five years; and the bank wanted him back.

He returned to Park Gate in some style. Like everyone else who had served in the forces, he received a demobilization allowance of one hundred pounds. He was given a blue suit with broad chalk stripes, a shirt, two collars, two pairs of socks, a pair of cuff links, a tie, and a brown trilby hat—all remarkably good quality, as if the ministry responsible for these matters had decided to redress the end-of-war failures of many previous conflicts (soldiers let go without pay and forced to beg, steal, or show their wounds for alms) by releasing to a relieved nation thousand of well-turned-out men, civilians once again. My father wore his demob suit to the bank for several years to come.

He returned, too, with a number of items that interested me, liberated from the Germans. Some were well-made mechanical objects: a handsome slide rule, whose use I never mastered, but which I liked to manipulate, bringing the rows of figures into new conjunctions; an infantry marching compass, with a mirror inside its matt-black lid that reflected the bearing you took on a distant point; and a portable typewriter, also black, made by the firm of Naumann-Seidel in Dresden—some of whose keys, like those for the vowels with umlauts and the German double ss, ß, were unused by us, but continued to insist on the machine's Germanness, and gradually, by subliminal association with efficiency, solid design, and productive work, helped change the way I felt when the word German was mentioned. At the time I was more taken with my father's largest trophy—a car. This was a Standard 10, a British make painted in German camouflage, which he had bought very cheaply—for £60—at an auction of goods repossessed from the defeated invaders of the Channel Islands. In Guernsey my father had had the use of a captured BMW, but he had decided that the much smaller Standard would be a better buy. Despite a back seat very much over the back axle, it had four doors, two per side hinged on a central column, with the front doors swinging backward. It had leather upholstery and walnut trim. The name may originally have been intended to prompt thoughts of the highest standards, but now suggested rather the idea of a norm that was modesty and austerity. A Standard 10, not a Daimler limousine, was used by Mr. and

Mrs. Attlee to drive to Buckingham Palace to be received by the King, when Mr. Attlee took over the reins of government in July 1945.

For some time my father drove his car around Park Gate and vicinity in its wartime colors—a faded jumble of grays, browns, and greens. Now and then former enlisted men who saw it pass gave the impression that it had required a last-minute effort to stop themselves springing to attention and saluting. A closer look, taken for example by pump attendants at garages selling Pool petrol (gasoline with proprietary names hadn't yet reappeared), brought forth questions about the origins of the car's paint scheme—no private-car owner in Britain had hitherto been known to have hoped to confuse Jerry air-raiders by painting his vehicle to look like a heap of dead leaves and grass cuttings. But after a while, when the novelty of driving a car with the appearance of a mobile compost heap had worn off—perhaps, too, when my father began to want to forget the army (though letters addressed to him as Captain Bailey continued to come for several years), or when he decided that preserving the German camouflage might be taken for some sort of demonstration of sympathy with the late enemy, or when, finally and most likely, he could afford to do something about it—he had the Standard resprayed. The garage that did the job had only one color to offer, a war-surplus aluminum. The result wasn't quite as shiny and new-looking as we expected it to be. However, it was a time when any sort of running car was hard to get: new models were just being advertised, but would be in short supply and not cheap, a Ford Prefect costing roughly £350. My father sold the Standard for £240 two years after bringing it back.

Sometimes—petrol coupons allowing—my father drove to work in Portchester, but generally he caught the train, now and then with me. The bank where he was employed was a small branch of the National Provincial, one of the five main British banks, for which he had worked since the age of seventeen: first in Southampton; then at the head office, in Bishopsgate, London; then in Portsmouth. Most of his friends were also "in the bank," men whose lives crisscrossed with his, working in Securities or Foreign Exchange at Bishopsgate or in county branches. Some remained good friends thereafter, like Cecil Burt, known as Burtie, who had been at Ryde School with him and was best man at his wedding; some were followed merely as names that appeared occasionally in the Staff Appointments listings in the bank's magazine.

Portchester's National Provincial occupied most of the ground floor of a two-story house, owned by the bank, on the corner of Castle Street and the main Portsmouth-Southampton road. It consisted of one large room with a counter and a small manager's office, with a leather-topped desk and a safe. Not much of value remained long in the safe, the day's cash being collected in the late afternoon and taken to Portsmouth. My father generally had one other person working with him. In the Dayton newspapers that reported my arrival there in 1940 I had been described as the son of a banker, or bank manager, but my father was then only a clerk-in-charge of a sub-branch; and that was the job he came back to after the war.

When we lived in the bank flat before the war, we entered the house through a side door in Castle Street. Our kitchen was downstairs; everything else upstairs. Banking hours were from ten until three, but this was for customers—my father was at work from nine till five-thirty, and later on Balance nights, when the previous half-year's accounts had to be worked out, or on occasions when the bank inspectors were going through the books. Sometimes during school holidays, before or after banking hours, I had entered the bank and looked at the ledgers, sat on the teller's stool behind the counter, and pretended I was paying out huge sums—well, hundreds of pounds. I had liked looking at my father's neat handwriting and figuring, sloping uniformly to the right. At his big desk I sat with my knees in the space between the tiers of drawers on each side and set the mahogany box calendar to the following day's date—it had a pair of knobs that wound on the months and the days, which then appeared—say, as DEC and 6—in small glass apertures, like the destinations on the fronts of buses. I had my own "Home Safe" account, of which I was proud, the Home Safe itself being a sort of steel piggy bank, book-shaped, which money could be put into but not got out of, except with the help of the bank manager who had the key.

My father, thus enmeshed for most of his working life in the handling of money, later confessed to me that he had never been very good at arithmetic. My mother, soon after their marriage, had persuaded him to study for the exams of the Institute of Bankers, which he managed to pass. But he was good at the public side of banking, befriending local tradespeople and businessmen who opened accounts or wanted to borrow money, and giving advice to elderly ladies on how to secure their skimpy funds. He had a shrewd common sense that was valuable in the job. Toward the end of his banking career, when he was the manager of a large branch in Brighton, he was approached for a hefty loan by a group who were among other things into pig-farming and sausage-making. The first step my father made was to go to a nearby shop and buy a pound of the sausages and take them home, where my mother fried them for lunch. My father was a connoisseur of sausages, or "bangers," as they were called. He decided that they were awful, and the requested loan was refused. Not long after he heard that a rival bank along the road had made the loan, and he wasn't surprised to hear a few months later that the firm (for which George Sanders, the actor, was a figurehead chairman) had gone bust.

My father's banking life had begun in Southampton, at a large branch of the National Provincial just below the Bargate. Mr. Edward Lancaster, the manager, wore wing collars and a frock coat, was a bachelor, and lived in the Polygon Hotel, Southampton's best hostelry. On Balance Nights, June 30 and December 31, when the entire staff was busy preparing the accounts for transfer to head office, he brought in champagne for everyone. The amount of paperwork and penwork then needed in banking was immense. My father recalled on some days being surrounded by a wall of customers' passbooks, in which every transaction had to be entered. All cheques—that is, checks!—had to be listed and sorted in three piles: one for checks going to county banks, one for local banks, and one for London banks.

For a while my father was seconded by Mr. Lancaster to a sub-branch that operated one day a week at a village called Hedge End, several miles out of town, to which my father generally rode on his Rudge motorcycle, carrying a large sum in cash on his pillion. The sub-branch was a front room in a house belonging to an elderly lady. In the strawberry season a large amount of money was paid in at the weekly opening by local growers. One June 30 Mr. Lancaster supervised the Southampton balance and then, at 11 P.M., rather the better for champagne, told my father they were going to do the balance at Hedge End. They got into a taxi, drove out to Hedge End, woke the rather startled lady of the house, and made a thoroughly ineffectual attempt to get the Hedge End books to balance.

Mr. Lancaster was responsible for recommending that my father be transferred to the bank's head office in Bishopsgate, where for five years he worked mostly in

Stocks and Securities. He made some extra money, as did all the Securities staff, buying new issues of stock on margin. During that time my father, still a bachelor, lodged in Stanstead Road, Catford, in southeast London, fairly close to the bank's sports ground in Lower Sydenham, where he trained and ran; a season ticket between the Lower Sydenham and Cannon Street stations gave him cheap travel to work, home, and sport. Trams screeched along Stanstead Road at all hours but he learned how to sleep through the noise. Every weekend he went down to Southampton to court my mother; although he had to work on Saturday mornings, he generally got away in time to catch a pre-noon train from Waterloo station. Eventually he got fed up with city life and told those in charge that he would like to be transferred to the south coast again, as he was getting married. A week before the great day he was posted to Portsmouth, from which, a few years later, he was sent out to take charge of Portchester. "Many of my pals in Securities went on to top jobs. One became general manager of the bank. It was the place to be," he once told me. But I don't think he regretted the move.

Except at balance times, or when the inspectors were about, my father never seemed to be unduly anxious about banking matters. He maintained that a mistake one day on the debit side was usually and naturally corrected by a mistake on the credit side the following day. "I never worried about a few pounds one way or another," he said. On the other hand, faced with customers who were cavalier in their financial behavior, he became quite rigorous. Persian students, for example—who studied at language schools and formed part of the cosmopolitan Brighton scene—often annoyed him. Most had collateral for their overdrafts in the shape of inexhaustible parental funds at home, but repayments from these sources could be obtained only after many letters and telegrams—and nudges to my father from head office. The fact that, under a phlegmatic surface, my father really did worry about banking matters became clear to me only many years later, when he was retired from the bank but still dreamed about it. Indeed, he considered a nightmare one dream in which he found himself behind a bank counter, faced with an impatient customer who produced stack after stack of bills to deposit, and which my father, proceeding to count, found were not pounds but a bizarre assortment of foreign currencies—dollars, rubles, dinars, zlotys, marks, francs, and pesetas, all jumbled together.

However, the bank was good for sport. As a young man my father ran for the bank, rowed for the bank, swam and played tennis for the bank. (It was at a tennis tournament in Southampton that he had met my mother.) His track victories, albeit modest provincial ones, made him in my eyes someone like Harold Abrahams or Lord Burghley, two distinguished British runners of the time. He was a keen local cricketer, playing for the Swanwick and Portchester elevens, his baggy white flannels held up by an old tie threaded through the waist loops. (In later years I was always happy to receive hand-me-downs from his sporting wardrobe—and still occasionally wear with pride his moth-holed blue Kent running shirt and a thin white cricketing sweater with a dark blue and light blue band around the collar.)

It was hard to fit into the same picture knowledge he later divulged. Roughly in his mid-twenties, the *victor ludorum* was beset by what he called phobias: he thought their onset may have had something to do with having his tonsils "snipped off" at the age of twenty-five, without even a local anesthetic, so it seemed, and giving him a long-lasting shock. Thereafter he found it hard to ride in lifts or elevators or look down from heights. He wouldn't climb the keep of Portchester Castle. Having to ascend the Welsh mountain of Snowdon during army wartime training, he kept his eyes fixed on the haversack of the man in front of him. In hotels, he requested rooms on the ground floor or lowest possible floor. In trains, he needed to sit in compartments with a corridor, if available (perhaps being locked in with his family on the train ride to Brighton had something to do with that). But despite these facets of character that were eventually revealed, I retained a vision of my father as fearless.

With his return from the war, my mother no longer concentrated her anxieties on Bridget and myself. After several years of being cooped up alone with first one child and then two, trying to "make do," "make ends meet," "put up with it," and generally "cope," as most people were struggling to do, she must have been very happy to have him home. Apart from the pleasures of the married state resumed, there was the simple delight of having an adult companion again: someone to share some of the responsibilities (which school should Bridget go to next year?) and make some of the decisions (should Tony see a doctor again about his feet?); someone to carry in the coal, peel the potatoes, and make her a cup of tea in the mornings. My father's renewed presence was brought home to us by sound as well as sight; wherever he was in the house, snatches of singing, humming, or whistling came from him—in the bathroom, in the kitchen, as he went out to the garden or to answer the bell at the front door. Usually they were fragments of songs—with a line or two recognizable—currently being broadcast by Vera Lynn, "the Forces' Favourite," or Anne Shelton, or by the duo Anne Ziegler and Webster Booth; songs like "I'll See You Again." Often it seemed as if my father was playing a part in a never-ending, impromptu, one-man opera, whistling, humming, and singing between pieces of talk. As he put on his coat and trilby in the morning I heard one of his most frequently sung snatches—"Hi ho, hi ho, it's off to work we go"—a line from the song of the Seven Dwarfs in the film *Snow White,* giving vent to which may have been an unconscious way of boosting his own morale as he set off for the bank. Much of the time I don't think he was aware that he was singing.

# 8

ONE WINTER EVENING TWO YEARS AFTER I CAME BACK to England, I walked up Duncan Road from Swanwick station, my satchel on my back, jumping over some puddles, skirting others. A man in a brown raincoat appeared, walking alongside me. He asked where I went to school and what sort of homework I had to do. We passed the strawberry-basket factory, with its great stacks of timber, and came to the place where the road bent as it went up the hill, with dark bushes and shrubs on one side. The nearest street lamp was a long way up the road. The man said, "I need to have a pee." Then he added some words to the effect that it would help if I had a pee too, standing beside him. He spoke in a mild-mannered way, as if it was an entirely natural, plausible suggestion. He unbuttoned his fly, pulled forth his member, and turned to look at me, his heavily shadowed face expressing the yearning that I do the same. I was standing at the edge of the road a few yards uphill of him. I didn't need to pee. I undid a few buttons and was putting in my hand to pull the thing forth to be agreeable when suddenly the whole business struck me as strange. I said, "I don't really need to. I think I'll be getting on home." And I did up the buttons again and hastened the remaining hundred yards to the gate of Edenholme. As I climbed the steps I looked down the road but I couldn't see him; perhaps he'd gone down the lane to the station again.

I didn't mention this incident to my mother. Obviously there was something not quite proper about it that penetrated my twelve-going-on-thirteen-year-old shell. I had some idea of the facts of life, thanks to information Debbie Spaeth had imparted to T.S. and me one afternoon in the front garden of 630 Runnymede, but I had little notion of further implications. I hadn't thought of urinating as being dubious or "dirty" in any way. In Ohio I had begun to realize that girls might be interesting in a way that was unlike the interest I took in other things—this new development had manifested itself in telephone calls to Marilyn Sargent and attempts to attract a smile from Dricka Haswell. But I hadn't linked this behavior with the little I knew about sex. Otto had delivered an avuncular warning to me one evening when I was in the bath about the desirability of having "clean thoughts," a recommendation that didn't make much immediate sense to me—it was hard enough getting one's ears, neck, and knees clean enough to please adults.

I was in the bath at Park Gate, scrubbing myself haphazardly with a face flannel and Lifebuoy soap (no longer a washcloth and Ivory soap), when the diminutive appendage between my legs began to behave in an astonishing way. I wondered for a moment if something was dreadfully wrong—would it pop? On the other hand, the feeling was pleasurable. As it grew to a handsome size, I looked at it with pride. This, clearly, was a prick—the word used by older boys at school but never till now meaningful to me. I felt a deep heaviness that was fine and at the same time a buoyancy (perhaps the bath water helped) and expectancy: what was going to happen would be wonderful. For a second or so it was; then, of course, the letdown.

But the event opened my eyes to happenings that had been going on all around me. Such as those occasions in school, perhaps on a warm summer afternoon when one might be feeling a drowsy, weighted sensation in the back of the neck, perhaps in a geography lesson in the midst of a tedious disquisition about Pre-Cambrian formations, when the master would suddenly shout: "Sykes! Get your hand out of your pocket and up on your desk!" And the curious, at once fierce but dreamy, expression on Sykes's face would be quickly replaced by a look of horrified embarrassment. Those of Sykes's knowledgeable classmates sitting near him in the back row would sneak a glance to see just how much of a bulge there was inside his trousers—or, indeed, if there were any telltale dark damp stain on the gray flannel alongside the fly. The back row was the place to be for that sort of thing. Sometimes two or three of the half dozen boys sitting there seemed to be lounging back, their knees pressed up under their desks, and with looks of unusual concentration. A master wanting to throw one of them into a complete panic would say, "Watson—perhaps you'd come up to the front and draw for us on the blackboard your impression of a rhomboid"—and Watson would say, after a gasp, "Yes, sir—just a moment, sir," lifting his desk lid and pretending to look for something; then get very slowly to his feet, possibly holding an exercise book in such a way as to conceal the now subsiding protuberance beneath his snake-buckled elastic belt; walk forward, ignoring a whispered comment from someone by the aisle: "Wanker Watson!"

None of the masters actually stood up and said, "There will be no masturbation in class." None of them told us that it would make us blind, daft, or cause our hair to fall out at a youthful age. But we got the impression there was something shameful about it, not to be openly discussed. (The word masturbation, like fornication, is ugly, and perhaps part of the trouble, the load imposed on it.) In my own case, this impression was reinforced by Father Frawley, the parish priest in Fareham, for whom I served at 10 A.M. Mass on Sundays as altar boy and to whom I went for confession. Father Frawley had already several times asked through the grilled window dividing us, "And were there now any occasions of self-abuse?" and had seemed a little disappointed with my reply, "I don't think so, Father" (not knowing quite what he was talking about). He then handed down a mild, routine sentence for me to say—together with an Act of Contrition—three Our Fathers and five Hail Marys as penance for my admitted one lie and one act of anger that week.

Now I knew. Wanking—also known as tossing off—was self-abuse! It was a sin—whether venial or mortal was not clear, perhaps fortunately; I knew that a mortal sin invited the pains of hellfire. At any rate I confessed to this sin now, though rarely with absolute honesty, often tacking it on to my list of confessed wrongs: "Oh—and bad thoughts and self-abuse—one or two times..." To which Father Frawley (who looked like Friar Tuck) would respond, knowing full well that his altar boy young Tony Bailey was on the other side of the confessional but maintaining the fiction that the confessee was anonymous, "You must try to control these lustful urges, my son." So it was turned into a struggle within oneself, set against a backdrop of secrecy and guilt, whereby one sought this much vaunted goal of Self Control, fighting the Lustful Urges, and of course often at last giving in (did the struggle make the surrender more pleasurable?), acceding to what Father Frawley described as Pleasures of the Flesh. Once or twice, church setting the context, I wondered whether God the Father in creating God the Son in the shape of a normal man had allowed Him, as a boy, to experience this sort of thing; but I didn't think it was the kind of question I could put to Father Frawley.

Although this pubertal impulse lacked, for a long time, any connection in my mind (or wherever lustful urges are bred) with girls, it did seem to be provoked by pictures of women one saw in print, and in words one read about them. My mother got magazines which I sometimes smuggled into my bedroom. With sheets and blankets pulled over my head, my chromed torch switched on, I turned the pages of Woman's Home Companion and admired the models in underwear. There was something very exciting even about such brand-names as Gossard and Kayser-Bondor. So an idea of female anatomy came in idealized form. And when I was replete with such images and the Bad Thoughts they induced, I sometimes read some of the fiction the magazines carried, stories about reckless women and masterful men that gave an overexcited, one-dimensional view of romantic entanglements between "grown-ups."

The main trouble with these growing pains, when you are amidst them, is that you have no sense of being part of the general life process. You don't imagine that this confused state of lust and remorse exists intermittently in the mind and body of just about every other thirteen-year-old boy in Park Gate, in Hampshire, in all of England. Even when the evidence is before you, as it was daily in and out of school, that you are one of many, you go on feeling alone and singular. Often it felt very depressing.

The girl I was interested in at this time didn't look anything like the women wearing nylon slips and silk stockings in the magazines. She was wearing when I first encountered her a dark-green school dress called a gym slip, wool stockings, and flat-heeled shoes; her name was Heather. She rode the train to Fareham, where she went to Wykeham House School, and she was usually on the train with several schoolmates when I got on in the mornings. Sometimes I found myself in their giggling proximity. Once, actually in the same compartment, I heard her name. I learnt that she lived in Bursledon, towards Southampton, on the slopes above the Hamble river. Several Saturday afternoons I made journeys from Park Gate in that direction.

The first Christmas my father was at home again—that of 1946—had been made additionally memorable by a present that wouldn't fit in a pillowcase: a bicycle. It was a Hercules, cost £9, and since chrome hadn't reappeared was finished entirely in black paint. But it had Sturmey-Archer gears, and I fitted it out with front and rear lights and a canvas saddlebag. In this I carried a raincoat, spanner, and puncture repair kit. Pretty soon I'd saved enough pocket money to replace the straight black handlebars with dropped handlebars in matt aluminum. Hercules bicycles were made in Aston, Birmingham—the home also of BSA bikes; other makes then slowly returning were New Hudson, Aberdale, Sunbeam, Raleigh, Rudge, Royal Enfield, Humber, Norman, Phillips, and Armstrong. The Hercules delighted me. It was much more fun to ride than the fat balloon-tire Schwinn, with an imitation motorcycle fuel tank and rear coaster brake, which I'd used in Dayton. On the Hercules I could change gears and get up speed and pretend I was a racing cyclist. With near-Herculean power I stood on the pedals as I climbed the hills. Going downhill from Sarisbury Green toward the Hamble River I swooped as if I were the immortal son of Zeus, feet not needing to turn, trying throughout the long curving descent to resist the cowardly temptation to squeeze the brake levers, wind shifting my hair, my back parallel with the road, my head down but my eyes upturned to watch the road ahead, especially potholes or sunken draincovers that could pitch me over the handlebars.

I freewheeled as far as I could at the bottom of the hill. I had to start pedaling again as I passed Moody's boatyard and went over the bridge across the Hamble. On the other side I turned into the steep, branchy network of lanes that led me toward old Bursledon church and the junction where, behind high hedges, stood the house in which—if I had my information right—Heather lived. I had no idea what I meant to do when I got there. She didn't know I was coming. I hoped that I would see her walking down the narrow road, or maybe cycling too. "Fancy meeting you! How about cycling over to Warsash with me?" I prepared various opening remarks as I puffed along. I approached the place slowly—the tall, tiled roof of the house became apparent through the trees—the driveway opened onto the road—I glanced in and saw nothing: no car, no people, no Heather. I rode by. I took a swing around the lanes, thinking Heather, Heather—thinking that if I thought hard enough about her she would materialize. I rode past the house again. Same thing—empty graveled drive and empty garden. Impelled by disappointment and a feeling of foolishness, I pedaled strenuously home.

"Had a good ride?" asked my mother.

"Not bad," I said, cross with myself for sounding cross.

"You look as if you could do with a nice cup of tea."

"All right." Didn't she know I really didn't like tea!

# 9

LONDON WAS A PLACE I READ ABOUT; MY FATHER ONCE a year went there for bank dinners. My metropolis was Fareham, and going there daily to school didn't spoil for me its urban allure. In fact Fareham was merely a market town with the usual quota of county council offices, building societies, estate agents, and banks. Shops ran along West Street: Stead & Simpsons, Timothy Whites, Macfisheries, Boots, Woolworths . . . West Street was wide—it had originally been two streets, and the intervening row of houses had been pulled down, making a space that was used most days for car-parking and on several days for market stalls. At its eastern end, High Street joined it from the north, with brass plates of solicitors and insurance agents alongside Georgian doorways. The railway station at the western end of town was one focus of interest, and the bus station was another (what wouldn't have interested me at the time was the fact that the novelist William Thackeray had spent childhood holidays in a house that had been pulled down for the bus station.) Here various routes of the Hants and Dorset Company, which had an empire to the west, met those of the Southdown Company, whose domain was to the east. The long-distance coaches of the Royal Blue Company ran from it in many directions. When we moved from Park Gate back to Portchester in 1947, to a house near the south end of Castle Street, it was more convenient to take a bus than a train to school. I became a rider of Southdown buses—hedge-green double-deckers. I hopped aboard the open platform at the rear and dashed up the stairs, hoping to find a seat at the front. Upstairs could be full of cigarette smoke, but it was the work of a moment to wind down the thin upper section of window, letting in a quartering gale that blew the Woodbine and Players fug to the rear, buffeted people's hair and hats, and caused a few passengers to mutter. In the front seats one felt the motion more—the forward onrush under overarching trees; the sideways tilt as the driver threw his machine into a right-angled bend out of White Hart Lane and leveled up for the cruise along Fareham Road. Downstairs—if there was no room on top—I was often sandwiched in with old people, mothers and babies, and would have to stand in the aisle clutching the chrome rail on the back of a seat while the conductor squeezed past with his change pouch and ticket machine. The platform being out of bounds, the best place to stand was right up front, on the right, where I could see the driver's back and his elbows moving as he turned the wheel, changed gear, or stuck his right hand out of the window to indicate that he was pulling out or making a turn. The best seats downstairs were the four-person seats at the rear, one on each side parallel with the aisle, on which—space permitting—one could slide back and forth, impelled (or pretending to be so) by the acceleration or braking of the bus. Certain items of bus hardware fascinated me, in that unexceptional way things have when you see them every day: the green leatherette curtain which the driver after dark pulled behind himself to prevent glare from the interior lights striking his windshield; the white concave button—for signaling the driver to halt at the next stop—inset in a disc marked PUSH ONCE; and the rough-surfaced metal plates, fastened to the backs of upstairs seats, on which smokers were meant to stub out their cigarettes. In Fareham bus station, I watched the drivers turn the outside handles that moved the rollers holding a reel of destination names; the geography of that part of Hampshire would flash past before one spot was fixed—Bedhampton, for example, or Southsea. A separate, smaller aperture indicated an interim resting place, as the Theatre Royal or Hilsea Garage.

More or less opposite the bus station stood the Embassy cinema, whose marquee advertised in black removable letters present and forthcoming attractions: *Frenchman's Creek,* with Joan Fontaine and Arturo de Cordova; Jennifer Jones in *Duel in the Sun* ("Lust in the Dust," it was quickly christened); and British films starring Patricia Roc, Phyllis Calvert, Jack Hawkins, and the wonderfully shifty and smirking Alistair Sim. Here, after watching Walt Disney's *Fantasia,* or a film about the RAF called *Target for Tonight,* we stood for the national anthem—a ritual one was exposed to more in the cinema than anywhere else. Behind the bus station was the street that led to Father Frawley's Sacred Heart church, a dour-looking, barn-shaped edifice constructed of rough gray stone, where we stood, sat, and kneeled. The street then ran down to the creek. Here the Jutes had landed; here the Danes had raided. Now there were a gasworks, a railway viaduct, and various scrappy buildings and workshops, between which one could glimpse the mud of the creek. In my memory, Fareham Creek always appears with the tide out.

For a long period I spent most of my spare time in Fareham at the railway station, quite apart from passing through it on the way to and from school. During the war I'd been in love with planes. I'd cherished differences of tail and wing shape, whether weapons were cannon or machine guns, engines radial or inline; every distinction that made for definition set up obscure vibrations of pleasure. Now it was trains. As with the warplanes, I wasn't alone in this. For the train-worshiping fraternity, made up mostly of boys between twelve and fifteen, numerous publications were produced; the one I generally carried in a jacket pocket was a booklet listing the numbers and names, when appropriate, of all the locomotives of the Southern Railway. (It became the Southern Region of British Railways when the four great railways—SR, GWR, LMS, and LNER—were nationalized and merged in January 1948.) The booklet was organized in categories of engine wheel arrangements—for example, 2–6–2, indicating that there were six large driving wheels between two smaller wheels at front and rear. The Lord Nelson class of Southern Railway engines was 4–6–0, as was the King Arthur class.

On reaching the station, I would purchase a penny platform ticket and then take up a position at the end of one of the central platforms. I preferred the northwest end, where I could see the junction of the three lines coming in from Southampton, Eastleigh, and Wickham. There I could get an early sight of smoke from the engine that hauled passenger carriages or goods wagons (in Dayton we would have said freight cars) toward me. Some of the goods trains shuffled slowly through, giving me ample time to gaze at the engine, wave at the engine driver, and write down in a notebook the engine's number, later to tick it off in the printed train-spotter's listing booklet—the vaguely determined goal being, presumably, to see and tick off every Southern Railway engine. Some, however, were pulling expresses, and for a moment or two the excitement of seeing and hearing the train, say the 2:32 from Plymouth to Brighton, rushing through Fareham station, smoke shooting up and around the roof of the platform, steam from the pistons billowing over the platform edge, was superimposed on the need—also a matter of excitement—to observe and note the engine's identity, hoping all the while that it wasn't one I'd seen before. "Sir Sagramore!" I had seen the Green Knight, Melisande, and

Joyous Gard. But Sir Sagramore was among those King Arthur class locomotives that still formed part of my train-spotter's grail—as were Elaine, Morgan le Fay, King Pellinore, Sir Blamor de Ganis, and Excalibur itself. I now wonder what small boy persisting inside a serious-looking railway official had the splendid thought of celebrating fragments of the British past in this way. Some of the past was not very distant, and history and heroes were joined by topography and well-known institutions. The Battle of Britain class, then just making an appearance, had engines named Croydon, Biggin Hill, Fighter Command, 75 Squadron, and Winston Churchill. Lord Nelson shared his class with Frobisher, Howard, Anson, and Collingwood. The Merchant Navy class generously allowed its honors to be borne by foreign shipping companies, too: United States Lines, Rotterdam Lloyd, and French Line CGT appeared in the list with Shaw Savill, Blue Star, British India Line, and Union Castle; companies whose vessels—with their funnels painted in distinguishing bands—I'd seen in Southampton docks or, at a greater distance, steaming out across Sandown Bay. I managed to be fond even of the dowdy engines of the River class, some of whom might have driven the devotee to detailed map reading in search of the Cuckmere, Rother, and Torridge. I was fascinated by the locomotives of the Schools class—chunky, powerful 4–4–0s—even though Price's wasn't there with Eton and Harrow, Stowe and Radley.

Not long ago I sat on a British Airways flight next to a young man who was clearly happy to be in a window seat. He held a small notebook, and as our Jumbo taxied away from the terminal he jotted down the registration numbers of every plane he could see. So the mania still exists, in slightly different form. I admit that I found it hard to imagine what would lead one to list various Tri-Stars, DC-10s, 747s, Tridents, and Super Caravelles. The excitement of being a train spotter could still be retrieved, but somehow wasn't transferable. Indeed trains still stir my emotions. Where my parents live now in retirement, in the New Forest, the main London-Southampton-Bournemouth line passes half a mile away, beyond some fields and a river, and when I hear a train I am drawn to the living-room window to watch it whizzing past the gaps in the distant clumps of trees, even though it is all-electric, each train more like the last than peas in a pod. In Stonington, Connecticut, where I lived fifteen years ago, I stood for an hour by the so-called shoreline of the New York, New Haven, and Hartford Railroad, shortly thereafter to become part of the Amtrak system, while waiting for the sight of a train. Not the indigenous Minuteman, Senator, or disappointing Turbotrain. This was to be the Flying Scotsman—an LNER locomotive that some American financial magnate had bought and was taking to Texas under its own steam. I stood on the derelict platform of Stonington station and waited, listening. I intended somehow to slow it down in my mind as it passed and take in every detail. Then I heard it coming. It was hooting for the ungated road crossing at Walker's Landing. It appeared around the bend by the Velvet Mill—the round cylindrical boiler; the tubby funnel; the slanting windows of the driver's cab—all quite small, really, by American scale—small bursts of steam—moving fast. I waved to the engine driver. He waved. But my eyes were altogether too misted over for me to catch the details as I'd planned.

# 10

WHEN THE U.S. GOVERNMENT HAD ABRUPTLY HALTED ITS Lend-Lease aid program to Britain at the end of the war, Britain owed the United States a huge dollar debt that—with much British overseas investments sold off and industrial recovery in the uncertain future—was clearly going to require patience from the creditor. For a few years then it was as if the U.S.A. once again seemed to be packing up its foreign troubles in an old kit bag and jettisoning them in Europe. The Yanks withdrew into their own thriving, continental fastness—drawing with them only such booty of war as the G.I. brides. But Uncle Joe's Russia was gradually perceived as the menace; Europe was needed, and had to be saved. In June 1947 an offer was made of American aid under the Marshall Plan. For Britain it came at the right moment, at the end of that third long winter and spring of freezes and floods, food shortages and power cuts. American generosity and common sense won out over American suspicion of the world and of foreign entanglements. On the British side, feeling about the U.S. reflected the fact that we were so deeply in debt we might never be able to pay it back. It made the British resentful, evasive, and sometimes overassertive.

My connection with America blossomed every now and then in the shape of a parcel from the Spaeths: care packages of food; clothes for my mother and Bridget; small Christmas presents and birthday gifts for me. And trends and proceedings in Anglo-American affairs were commented on in Otto Spaeth's occasional letters to me.

Otto, of Bavarian ancestry, was not at all an isolationist; he had a view—at once idealistic and commercial—of an interdependent world. Among other things, America needed European markets for its products. And God approved of nations, like neighbors, doing unto others as they would have others do unto them. The war had been good to Otto. His machine-tool factory won war production honors for fulfilling large orders efficiently and rapidly; but with the peace he began to lose interest in the tools by which he made money and he became more preoccupied with art, particularly liturgical art, and in the politics of the area where art and religion overlapped. It was natural that Dayton no longer seemed the place best suited to Spaeth life. Eloise, moreover, was bored with living there, though she had stuck with it while necessary and had enlivened its artistic life through exhibitions she had mounted at the modern wing of the Art Institute. She and Otto invited me over to spend with them what was to be their last summer in 630 Runnymede.

My other American connection remained my godfather, Roy Bower, for whom my mother had worked as a secretary at the American Consulate in Southampton in the late 1920s. Roy, a bespectacled bachelor, had been stationed in Munich when war broke out in 1939, and had visited me twice while I was with the Spaeths. He was now American consul in Madras, India. I wrote to him there and letters continued to come from him, nicely mixing praise and criticism for the way I wrote and drew, and letting me know that he, too, had been floored by math—however, he had managed to get the minimum grade; the suggestion was that I could also. "It's like measles," wrote Roy. "You might as well have it and get it over with." And Roy saw my connection with the Spaeths in a way that was so unusual I didn't take it very seriously: this was that *I* had been good for *them.* "I am glad that you keep up with the Spaeths," he wrote. "They have so much to be grateful to you for. A chance to be kind, among other things. And a chance to appreciate the stuff a young Briton is made of."

This might have been entered in the category of remarks one made in the hope that by making them they would become true; but Roy didn't leave it at that. He wanted to know what I was reading—had I read *Cranford?* If not, I had a treat in store. Furthermore, he had asked a book club to send Bridget and me six books each at intervals during the year to come. It was called the Golden Hour Book Club, which he thought a sloppy name, and he was afraid that it might send books that were too young for me. He was reminded of the occasion when Bernard Shaw had been asked to subscribe to the foundation of a children's library in Portsmouth in honor of Charles Dickens (whom Roy didn't need to tell me had also been a Portsmouth boy). Shaw said that he'd be glad to subscribe if the library would guarantee to stock only those books children liked to read, such as the works of Charles Dickens and Bernard Shaw. Roy had lived as a child in Spokane, Washington, where, despite its being what he called "just an overgrown mining and lumbering town," most of his high school class had read "all the classics" by graduation, and some—including him—continued to keep up with contemporary literature—for example the works of Barrie, Galsworthy, W.J. Locke, and John Masefield. Roy, needless to say, was an Anglophile. There was a donnish friendliness in the voice that came through his writing. But his typing had begun to be erratic; his eyesight was going, a symptom of the illness that led him to retire early from the Foreign Service and brought about his death in 1950.

The Golden Hour Book Club was in fact a success. Several of the books made a lasting impression on me.

One black-bound volume, published by what struck me as the strangely named firm of Liveright in New York, was *The Story of Tolerance,* by Hendrik van Loon. This was a partisan and didactic account of the progress through the ages of what might now be called human rights, and fragments stayed in the mind with the help of van Loon's spiky pen drawings. These showed saints being martyred, Luther nailing his theses to the door of Wittenberg Cathedral, and the Declaration of Independence being signed in Philadelphia—or was it William Penn founding the city of brotherly love?

There was one other strand of the "special relationship"—as politicians later referred to the tie between the U.K. and U.S.A.—that concerned me, and that was a part of my Bailey heritage. Grandpa Bailey had been to the States as a young man. For a long time I believed that he had been a cowboy in Montana; and the word "Montana," describing a place I had never seen, summoned up a high landscape of bluffs and mesas, with herds of bison, packs of Indians in feathered headdresses, and the occasional lone cowboy protecting his cattle. With this belief and the associated images was connected another idea—that my grandfather had brought back from his stay in the West a splendid Mexican saddle, decorated with silver. At one point in the 1970s, in the course of a family celebration in a Ventnor, Isle of Wight, hotel, I managed to get my father and my uncle Jim to talking about the Bailey family (in a way that separately they were reluctant to talk), and one or other of them alluded to the year that their father had spent working on a farm in Virginia.

"But what about Montana?" I said. "Wasn't he a cowboy there?"

"Good gracious, no," said Jim. "It was Virginia. An ordinary farm."

"And didn't he bring back a Mexican saddle?"

"I don't remember that," said my father.

"Neither do I," said Jim.

Oral history obviously has its moments of difficulty.

Otto cabled funds with which my father bought me a cabin-class ticket for the *Queen Elizabeth,* sailing from Southampton on July 24, 1947, arriving in New York on July 29. It was still natural (in fact remained so for roughly fifteen years) to think first of ships when considering a transatlantic journey. Plane flights took over twelve hours and went by way of Scotland, Iceland, and Newfoundland or Labrador. Comfort was something promised for the future. Articles in magazines like *Picture Post* described such aircraft as the Bristol Brabazon, then under construction, which readers were assured was going to provide eighty sleeper berths for overnight passengers across the ocean. Cutaway drawings showed a separate cocktail bar, lounge and dining salon, all apparently designed to make the traveler feel he was riding in a liner of the air. However, by the time a couple of Brabazons had been built, it was clear that great range, speed, and passenger capacity were going to be better qualifications for planes competing with ships on the transatlantic run. The Brabazon never went into series production; the original pair were sold for scrap in 1952.

I boarded the "Lizzie" (as I referred to her, with rather smug familiarity, in a letter home) as a two-voyage veteran of the Western Ocean. But she was huge compared with the *Antonia,* the Cunarder on which I'd crossed to Canada in 1940, or the escort carrier *Ranee* on which I'd returned. She had made her maiden civilian voyage in October the year before (carrying 2,288 passengers, among them the Soviet statesmen Molotov and Vyshinsky); the gray paint of her troop-carrying days was gone, the murals and carpets had finally been installed, and bouillon and biscuits were being served to passengers, wrapped in rugs, who relaxed in deck chairs while the great ship steamed westward. I was fourteen and less interested in the bouillon and rugs than in the ship itself, the largest passenger liner in the world, and all its facilities. I dashed from my berth, in a cabin shared with a young Cuban doctor who had been studying in Spain, to attend breakfast—I tried eggs cooked differently each morning, fried, scrambled, boiled, shirred, and poached. I swam in the pool, attended rumba lessons, wrote letters on the ship's stationery, read the ship's newspaper, played shuffleboard, went to lunch, marched around the decks, went to the cinema, played table tennis with the Cuban and an American army sergeant who had been serving in Germany, and went to dinner to sample the multiplicity of courses: Timbale of Ham; Médaillon of Veal Milanese; Halibut, Sauce Mousseline; Roast Shoulder of Lamb; Almond Pudding, Melba Sauce... This was the year in which Hugh Dalton, Chancellor of the Exchequer, halted the use of petrol for private purposes and the use of sterling for holidays abroad. To go abroad one had to be invited as a guest, without any ability to pay one's way, or resorted to various dodges, exchanging with one's hosts the provision of meals and lodging when abroad for the same in Britain. I was a favored person. I also felt like an Atlantic traveler. Perhaps if I hadn't made this trip, memory of the earlier crossings would have faded, and the ocean would have become to me what it was to many—a wide, almost impassable barrier. I stood at the rail and watched the bow wave of the ship crest outward, then upward in white spume where it collided with the seas, the horizon curving wide and unbroken. It seemed perfectly natural to be here, my feet braced slightly against the slow roll and dignified pitch of the liner, breathing the salt air—going from one country to another. With a bakelite Baby Brownie I recorded—in what turned out to be smudgy snaps of overdistant subjects—the *Queen Elizabeth*'s passage up New York harbor: the Statue of Liberty; a tall-funneled Moran tug; a Susquehanna ferryboat; and the long-fingered piers in the North River, somehow mimicked by the standing pillars of skyscrapers rising on Manhattan behind them.

A woman friend of Eloise's met me, took me to lunch at the Commodore Hotel, and put me on the overnight train to Dayton. Only three years before I had traveled with Eloise the other way, along the Erie and down the Hudson valley, but it seemed like a long time before. It was now a journey I could make unaccompanied. And when I saw 630 Runnymede again, I felt delight mixed with a slight dismay—once this huge, marvelous house had been my home! It was as if the extent of what had been given up on going back to England, never fully realized or allowed to surface in England, suddenly became clear to me. It was the first (but not the last) time I was conscious of the melancholy such a return brings about. Yet this was only an element in an alloy of feelings. Most of what I felt was excitement at seeing the Spaeths again.

Tony S. was now thirteen, Mimi seven. The two older girls were both away for the summer. Marna had been given a Chevrolet coupe as a college graduation present and had driven to Cape Cod with a friend. Debbie was at camp. (So were my old friends Harry and Fred. I missed seeing them, and also James, who was taking a vacation prior to going to work for the Haswells.) All the energy of life as led by Uncle Otto and Aunt Eloise, as I continued to call them, picked me up and swept me along. It seemed normal enough that a reporter would call, once I was back in the Spaeth orbit. The young woman assigned by the *Dayton Daily News* to cover Evacuee Returns asked, How does it feel to be back?—answer, Wonderful—and was, I afterward concluded, color-blind, since she wrote that I was wearing a blue serge suit when in fact I was in gray flannel. (Later, as a cub reporter myself, I found that it was just that sort of basic information one forgot to note at the time of the interview, and took a wild stab at over the typewriter.) Then it was off swimming with T.S. in the cold, spring-fed water of the pool at the Polo Club; off to lunch at Moraine Country Club, where Otto played golf with other Dayton industrialists and engineering geniuses, like Charles Kettering; off to Wright Field with Otto to look at the new Lockheed Constellation, and then with Eloise to an opening at the Art Institute. After a few days I noticed that T.S.—whose full name was Otto Lucien Anton Spaeth, Jr.—seemed to have developed his own way of handling the superhuman activity of his parents, having both a pride in them and their possessions (like Otto's billiard table, on which T.S. and his friends taught me to play pool), and a slightly self-effacing, self-preserving humor. It made me think of one of the stoical Romans in *Daily Life in Ancient Rome*—a Price's textbook that Ollie Johnston had our noses pressed into; one of those toga-clad citizens who managed to present an air of smiling, well-mannered calm while distant provinces were rebelling and volcanoes were erupting.

T.S., however, was as excited as Otto about the thirty-five-foot-long Greyhound bus that Otto had bought and was having fitted out as a land yacht. The largest of the gadgets Otto indulged in, it became his vehicle for cross-country jaunts, for expeditions to proselytize religious communities and commercial companies on the useful delights of modern art, and for tours that took him from one golf course to another. I described the Ottobus or Spaethship in my previous book about being in Dayton during the war, *America, Lost and Found,* but Eloise, reading that memoir, thought I hadn't done justice to the coach's role in propagating the faith of art-in-business and art-in-religion. She told me that on one occasion the bus carried the entire board of trustees of the American Federation of Arts (of which Otto had become chairman) to a meeting in Philadelphia. On the return trip to New York, Lloyd Goodrich, then director of the Whitney Museum, got into a violent argument with Francis Taylor, director of the Metropolitan Museum, and they had to be separated—a job effected by René d'Harnancourt, the six-foot-four-inch-tall director of the Museum of Modern Art. Eloise said, "On reaching New York, Taylor disembarked at Seventy-second Street and Park Avenue when he found that otherwise he'd be alone on the coach with Goodrich for the last twenty blocks."

After *America, Lost and Found* was published I also received a bus story in the form of a letter from a woman who said that my book had solved a mystery that had long bothered her and her husband. They had just been married—it was in the late 1940s; her husband, serving in the U.S. Navy, had been posted to Pensacola. They drove south and stopped one afternoon at Pinehurst, North Carolina, to watch Ben Hogan play in a golf championship. At dusk, as they returned to their car, they saw in the corner of the parking lot a bus that was clearly not an ordinary bus. Through one of the big side windows they looked in and saw a solitary man sitting at a table eating dinner, while another man waited on him. "We often wondered who this person was, and what he did," she wrote. "We are very glad to know." She and her husband had now retired and were living in a mobile motor home in which they toured the country.

The Ottobus, forerunner of so many Winnebagos and other recreational vehicles, was still being completed that summer I returned. I had to make do with a personal presentation from Otto, with slides and blueprints, showing how the bus was going to look, inside and out:

the triple stateroom forward; the midships galley, and bathroom, complete with bath; the lounge aft, with two couches that converted into bunks; the radio telephone; the paintings that would be hung on inner walls. And when we proceeded to make a journey to Illinois and Iowa to see Spaeth relatives, it was in a smaller vehicle: a black and gray Cadillac limousine. Tony S., Mimi, and I had the wide back seat, a large area of gray carpeted floor, and two small jump seats that folded out of the back of the front seat. Up front, Eloise sometimes took a turn at driving, but mostly she kept Otto entertained, as he drove, by reading to him snippets of articles from *Art News* or *Commonweal,* the liberal Catholic weekly. When she was at the wheel she drove with verve, enjoying it. (Many years later, when she was approaching her eightieth birthday, Eloise drove me to catch a ferry at Orient, Long Island. We were running a little late, and as we hurtled round a sharp bend near Sag Harbor Eloise said to me with a smile, comfortingly, "Otto taught me how to bank.") I watched the midwestern landscape unroll: the seemingly endless corn and alfalfa fields; the barns and silos, farmhouses and Burma-Shave advertisements. We had to stop now and then for Mimi, who got carsick. I also felt the motion, which was a bit like that of the *Queen Elizabeth,* a soft, cushiony sway (not at all like the ride of the Bailey Standard, which bottomed out hard at every bump). But this didn't stop me eating happily when Otto stopped at one of the burgeoning Howard Johnson's chain of restaurants. Otto had acquired the franchise to build and operate one in Dayton, and was anxious to see what fellow HoJo operators were up to. (Otto's restaurant, apparently ideally sited at the end of Far Hills Avenue in Oakwood, close to a movie theater and shopping center, turned out to be for some reason one of the few really poor investments he ever made.) T.S., Mimi, and I sampled some of Howard

Johnson's twenty-eight different flavors of ice cream. I came to the profound fourteen-year-old conclusion that even if food wasn't everything, here in the breadbasket of the world, amid half-pound hamburgers, club sandwiches, waffles with maple syrup, and pie à la mode, it provided a good reason for thinking that God had blessed America and all who ate in her.

We stopped in Decatur, Illinois, Otto and Eloise's hometown. Eloise long afterward told me that her mother had once said to her, "It's just as easy to marry a rich man as a poor one." But it was, Eloise thought, a pure fluke that she met and married Otto, for he had lived on one side of Decatur, she on the other. He went to the German Catholic church, she to the Irish. They might never have met, but when a touring film company came to town, as such companies did in those days, to make a film for and about the place—with local performers, a title like *The Spirit of Decatur* and, presumably, local audiences after it was made—Eloise was chosen to be the heroine. Otto was asked to lend the production his big Packard roadster. He wasn't asked to drive it, but came along to see it used. He then asked if he could take Eloise home; she said no, she already had a ride with a friend. But he called her the next night for a date, and that was that.

On our visit to Decatur, among Eloise's O'Mara relatives, and in Davenport, Iowa, where Otto's brother Bernard and his family lived, it was interesting to see that people could be close to the Spaeths and yet live in ordinary houses—large frame houses on tree-lined streets or modern homes in suburbs, but not at all on the grandeur level of 630 Runnymede. Among cultured old German-American aunts or go-getting young Iowan cousins, Otto continued to shine as the all-round wonderman—New York the next step, his star still rising. I was part of his entourage—"You remember young

Tony Bailey who stayed with us during the war?"—and happy to shine in his reflected glory.

Back in England via the *America*, the flagship of the United States Lines, I found it hard to explain to my school chum Peter Blewden (whose father ran a newspaper and tobacco shop in Portsmouth) what the short visit to the States had been like: swimming pools, pool tables, big cars, stores instead of shops—that was some of it, easily talked about. (Sparing his feelings, I didn't go on too much about the food. Britain at that point was in the midst of two years of bread rationing.) But there were other things that I felt in my bones but didn't quite know how to give expression to: the great space of the country; the buoyancy of the Spaeths, which seemed to hold one up higher out of the sea in which we were commonly, uniformly immersed; and a feeling that an American part of me had received a vital recharge.

The Bulova watch Eloise had acquired for me as I went aboard the *Ranee* had ceased to work a year before. I'd grown out of the knitted T-shirt with winged motif on the chest that I had worn when being drawn in 1943 by the artist the Spaeths had commissioned to portray all their children, including me. In time I lost the silver dollar that Orville Wright had given me. I resumed the English disposition and mostly English speech (underlaid for ever by a hint of an American accent) that Otto, during the war, had been afraid my parents would consider as lost for good. But within all this lay a deeply deposited and capacious reservoir that would eventually flood forth in transient likings for Old Gold cigarettes, the writing of Scott Fitzgerald, the singing of Doris Day, and other, as it turned out, longer-lasting loves.

# 11

A GREAT EXPLOSION GREETED MY FAMILY'S RETURN TO Portchester in 1947. It was not, as our new neighbours in Castle Street feared, the start of World War III; but as we stood outside amid fallen tiles and shattered windowpanes, word came that an ammunition barge moored a mile or so away in Portsmouth Harbor had blown up. Damage was done to houses over a wide area. The Admiralty paid compensation, and the roof of the house we had just moved into—a roof that had been in need of repair and restoration—was put right at government expense.

In the course of his banking career, my father generally found comfortable but unexceptional houses to live in. 172 Castle Street, rather coyly called Dovercot, was less ordinary. My father had managed to take over the lease from friends who were moving away from the area, and then discovered that the owners—two elderly ladies living in London—wanted to sell the house. So, with a 3 percent mortgage that was one of the benefits of working for the bank, he bought it. The main part of the house stood at a right angle to Castle Street, with a distinctive steep, red-tiled, barn-type roof, within which were two third-floor bedrooms, and whose height had exposed it to the shock wave of the explosion. Joined to this part of the house were a pair of old cottages, forming a wing, set back behind a small garden. The ground floor of the more distant cottage had been made into a garage. Above the garage lived an elderly man, who had been allowed to reside there rent-free by the charitable former Dovercot tenant. The smell in his room was a rank mixture of zoo and farmyard. The old man—called Elmy, the surname being all he offered—had at one time been a gravedigger; he seemed more like a tramp who had finally found a roost. He had apparently no relatives or connections; it was unclear what he lived on. My mother gave him Sunday dinner once a week. He was admitted to hospital about a year after we moved in, and when he died there my father arranged his burial. Elmy, perhaps, was a reason Dovercot had been for sale at a reasonable price.

I had the back bedroom up under the roof, with a view down the long garden to the trees that stood along the edge of a field backing onto Portchester Creek, a wide arm of Portsmouth harbor. I also had the use of an otherwise vacant room in the nearer cottage, which I used in turn for making model planes, chemistry experiments, and developing and printing photographs. For a couple of months I bought camera magazines, purchased the necessary trays and developers, put up some blackout curtains, and by the light of a 25-watt bulb painted red, watched misty prints form on the curled-up paper. Then I lost interest in the hobby. There was, come to think of it, something inherently off-putting in the word "hobby," suggesting that it was a part-time way of amusing oneself, inessential to real life.

It was curious that my parents left the cottages more or less as they found them. In the age of proud house-ownership and do-it-yourself rehabilitation few would be satisfied with this, but would put in bathrooms with local-government improvement grants and rent out the fancied-up accommodation. Perhaps the main part of the house seemed large enough for our domestic needs. Perhaps we didn't have the money. Perhaps, too, the unrestored rooms formed a buffer zone between the areas of relatively well-pulled-together Bailey family life and the pungent decomposition that was Elmy's.

On a beam in a back hallway at Dovercot I found a carved date—1732. The house was one of several dozen old brick buildings that made a nearly separate hamlet at the south end of Castle Street, roughly a mile from the center of Portchester, on the main Portsmouth-Fareham road. Opposite Dovercot was St. Vincent House, a handsome Georgian structure, inhabited quite appropriately—for a house named after a great naval battle—by a Royal Navy captain and his family. Next door to us, heading south, was Wistaria Cottage, where lived Mrs. Russell and her daughter, who both struck me as having a very posh manner. Beyond them stood Myrtle Cottage, the home of Commander Hamond and his wife, Mary. The Commander was one of the many ex-naval officers who lived roundabout and who had been "axed," that is, made redundant, fairly early on in their careers and were now working for local firms as executives and salesmen, or had taken up market gardening or helping run the local boy-scout troop. Commander Hamond had become a boat builder, and sounds of sawing and hammering came from a shed in Myrtle Cottage's garden. Across the road was a pub, the Cormorant, and a small tea shop, patronized by visitors to the Castle. This latter structure could be seen down the more easterly of the two lanes into which Castle Street forked—the tall gray tower of the Norman keep and the high walls of the medieval castle set in one corner of the Roman fort, which was surrounded by deep ditches, a moat, and a gently sloping, curving, earthwork.

What Talbott Hill, across the road from 630 Runnymede, had provided as a playground in Dayton, the Castle furnished here. The Roman walls, like eroded chalk cliffs, had crevices and protrusions that, up to a point, made them good for climbing. That point was about ten feet off the ground with me, when vertigo made itself felt and hand- and footholds seemed to disappear, leaving me frozen—at least in the eyes of my pals, standing below; a nervous quivering spread from the extremities into the core of my body, pressed against the old stone. After a pause for renewed strength and reconsideration of the descent, I edged my way down. Trembling limbs then recovered by kicking or knocking a ball around the wide grassy area within the walls. At the center of this was the pitch on which the Portchester cricket team, of which my father was a member, played their home matches. In one of the bastions a pavilion had been built, where the groundsman kept his mower, and from which he occasionally appeared, like Polyphemus from his cave, shouting at boys who looked as if they might be about to defile his precious turf. Other guardians of the place, part of the empire of the Ministry of Works, yelled at us for wall climbing. In the corner of the grounds diagonally opposite the Norman keep stood a Norman church and graveyard. Toward the southwestern corner there were impressions in the grass of the outlines of Saxon buildings, darker markings as with a photographic print that wouldn't quite come through, needing a stronger developer or much longer time.

Then, as with a great deal of what was put before me as I grew up, I took Portchester Castle mostly for granted. Only later did I realize that I'd had the good fortune to enjoy—tangibly and in that osmotic way that comes from being in a specific place, sitting on its grass, breathing its air, and gazing at its artifacts—one of the best-preserved Roman fortresses in Britain. It was immensely, purposefully square, each side about one hundred and eighty meters long, the walls some six meters high and three meters thick. The four corners were perfect right angles. It was a late Roman construction, built at a time when the barbarians were pressing hard against the imperial frontiers, and Frankish and Saxon pirates were raiding the Channel coasts. It was part of the defensive scheme of things taken over by the usurping military leader Carausius when he set himself up as emperor in Britain. The fort was integrated into the command of the Romano-British Count of the Saxon Shore, whose job was to protect the Channel coast from continental raiders. After a powerful barbarian attack in A.D. 367, the fort is thought to have been abandoned by the forces of Count Theodosius in favor of a site near Southhampton. It was there lying ready for Saxons who came to settle and who used it as a stockade within which their domestic buildings were secure; and it was available for Edward the elder, King Alfred's son, to form part of a national defence network against Viking attacks. The fort remained in good shape for the Norman occupiers of Britain. In its northwest corner a square-towered keep was built by the conquerors, three giant stories high, with its own enclosure of curtain walls—the inner bailey, as it was called, a term that gave me a strong feeling of kinship with the place. The castle was handy for Henry, one of William the Conqueror's sons, when he had himself proclaimed king on the death of his older brother William Rufus, quickly taking this step before the eldest brother, Robert, Duke of Normandy, got the news of William Rufus's death. Henry strengthened Portchester, using it—as did his heirs—as his embarkation port for crossing the channel to Normandy. In those days a great forest called Bere, of which a few scraps remain, lay across the back flanks of Portsdown Hill and afforded the Norman kings excellent hunting territory.

So here, just down the street, was a place where Roman soldiers had guarded the gates and the long Norse ships had been pulled up on the shore, a place that had been part of the lives of the kings who formed the long lists we had to learn in history lessons. Henry II had used

Portchester Castle to store his treasure and to confine important prisoners. Richard Coeur de Lion sailed from it at the end of his one short visit to England during his reign. John was often here, and Richard II modernized it, having the roofs covered with lead, drainpipes fitted, and tiles for firebacks imported from Flanders. The English troops who fought against the French at Crécy and Agincourt sailed from Portchester. In Tudor times it served as a military hospital; in succeeding wars it housed Dutch and French prisoners. During the Napoleonic wars five thousand French sailors lived in huts set up within the Norman bailey and the Roman enclosure; they kept themselves busy carving bone into buttons and ornaments, and inscribing their names on the old walls in spidery capital letters, the way one did who signed himself JOSEPH SOCHET.

I sometimes wondered about Sochet and his colleagues as I clambered over the masonry. I peered into deep spaces that had been dungeons in Norman times and thought with compassion and vicarious horror (which lasted all of a second) about those who had been confined there. I stood on the bastions and gazed down the harbor, imagining myself one of the last centurions of the faltering empire on the lookout for Saxon raiders. I could see the masts of Nelson's *Victory* in her dry dock at Portsmouth, beyond the mothballed World War II warships lying at their moorings. On Portsdown, to the north, an obelisk to Nelson stood against the skyline. Of course, other visitors often wandered round the Castle, and the local cricket matches and fêtes were held in the grounds, but much of the time it was deserted, except for a few contemporaries of mine. Within the gray-white stone walls enclosing green turf I was a count or seneschal. I guarded the king's prisoners. I was Joseph Sochet, planning to escape.

One evening after I had done my homework I headed for the door.

My mother asked, "Where are you going?"

"The Castle."

"Are you meeting friends there?"

I mentioned the names of several local lads, who I knew might be hanging around by the Water Gate. I didn't say that several local girls might be with them.

"Where do they live?" my mother wanted to know.

"Along White Hart Lane, I think." White Hart Lane was lined in part by houses owned by the local district council, where people lived who generally couldn't afford to buy their own homes.

My mother looked disappointed. She said, "You know, you should be careful whom you go around with. You have to think of your father's position."

It was my turn to look disappointed. I nodded, and dashed out of the door.

Coming back to England, I had come back to class. For four years I had been outside the system. Not that our Dayton suburb of Oakwood could have been claimed as typical of the American way—it was a place where, within the framework of American democracy, most people were quite well off, and the Spaeths were more so. However, among my friends at Harmon Avenue Grade School (a free school, by the way), there was no one who represented the extremes of wealth or poverty. If there were any danger of discrimination, it might have been one in which a comfortably middle and upper-middle income group, having very little contact with the poor, rejects (or feels uneasy with) the very wealthy. In fact, Tony Spaeth may have felt this more than I did, because I was an oddity, an outsider taken in for the war—a token of the alliance with Britain and of American hospitality to refugees; whereas T.S. had a cook, *and* a butler-chauffeur, *and* a governess. But by and large all Oakwood children shared a privileged life; their parents, buying an Oakwood house and thereby the right to send their children to Oakwood schools, made it unnecessary to think of private schools. One of my American grade-school contemporaries told me many years later that he and his friends who had grown up in Oakwood referred to it as The Dome—as if it were a greenhouse providing shelter from an unpleasant environment, where one was secure, and which one left only to return to as soon as one could.

I had in a way arrived in Oakwood thanks to class. One of the criteria governing the evacuation scheme on which I traveled to America was that it was intended to benefit the children of "professional and clerical" British families—I think the children of the clergy were what the scheme organizers had in mind, and not those of office assistants. (My father's title in 1940 was clerk-in-charge, but he was considered to be a member of the professional class.) The practical idea was to ensure that children were placed with families much like their own—and which, most importantly, could afford to house, clothe, and feed their young guests without hardship. In practice, some British evacuees were drastically misplaced—in Oakwood, for instance, the son of an impoverished Church of England vicar was taken in by a childless wealthy couple, in whose mansion he in no way felt at home. In my own case, living with the Spaeths, although eye-opening, was far from upsetting. Not until long afterward did I realize that many other British children of different social backgrounds and no American connections had been evacuated, if at all, from streets, say, in the East End of London to West Country villages or Welsh farms where things must have seemed as strange to them as Ohio did to me, if a good deal less enchanting and encouraging. In Britain, moreover, the small size of the country and the close packing together of people made it much harder to ignore the inequalities brought about by birth and background, and maintained by many a custom.

Certainly those four American years left me feeling slightly unsure of myself in Britain when dealing with both workers and toffs. It also made them unsure of me. They weren't able to place me. I wasn't to be precisely defined, as foreigner or native, and, within the classes, as upper, middle, or lower. Mostly I'm grateful for this escape from what seems to me a generally pernicious habit of categorization—a need to compartmentalize people, to decide a priori what can or can't be said to them or expected of them; a means of arranging society according to one's assumptions about it, a way of giving oneself less bother. But it results in the lessening of mobility, flexibility, and interaction—or it did so then, even more than it does today, after nearly forty years of the Welfare State. Poor Britain, poorer for those rigid demarcations. In the late 1940s there seemed to be an even greater distinction between those students who went to grammar schools and those who went to the ill-named "secondary moderns" than there was between expensively educated public-school students and those at grammar schools. My would-be companions loitering in the grounds of Portchester Castle, waiting without much hope for something to happen to invigorate their lives, were secondary modern kids, stuck in a proletarian present—for all their cocky behavior and blunt language ("sod" and "bugger" were considered bad words by the refined middle and upper classes)—captives of the Castle in different ways from me.

# 12

THE CASTLE WAS THERE BECAUSE OF THE CREEK. AND the creek, the northeastern arm of Portsmouth harbor, soon became the focal point of my existence. Getting up in the morning I would look out of my bedroom window for the fragmentary view through trees and across the meadow: gray water, brown mud, in proportions that varied with the tide. At low water there was a thin, barely perceptible trickle curving in a ditch through the brown expanse. At high tide the creek made a wide reflection of clouds and sky. I could tell whether the tide was flooding or ebbing from the direction in which the moored boats were pointing. Looking at the trees to see whether their branches were shaking or still, were waving gently or hysterically, I would gain early information about the suitability of the day for sailing. If the wind was due west I could smell the bone works that made glue, at Wicor, toward Fareham.

I'd learned the rudiments of sailing at summer camp on Torch Lake, in Michigan. But that was in a boat with several other eleven-year-olds, with an instructor who was most of all concerned that we learn to duck when the boom flew over and that we hung on when the boat heeled, putting our modest weights on the windward gunwale to keep the boat from tipping over and pitching us into the lake. The first lessons to absorb about sailing boats were that they could knock you unconscious and in one way or other get you soaking wet. In the next stage, at Portchester, Jonathan Rowe taught me. The elder son of a woman doctor, living a few houses away in Castle Street, he was a tall, reticent youth, a few years older than me, who later joined the regular army and became a tank officer. His father, rarely seen, ran a hotel in Devon. Jonathan had his own boat and though—as I now realize—he was a loner, no doubt preferring to sail by himself, he generously took me along as his crew on half a dozen occasions, made me take the helm, and showed me how to conduct the basic maneuvers of coming about and gybing. He demonstrated what happened when one luffed and the sails began to shake along their leading edges, and explained why one let out or pulled in the jib and main sheets on different points of sailing. Jonathan showed me where the centerboard should be positioned for beating, reaching, and running. He made me shoot the boat up into the eye of wind, losing way, in order to pick up the mooring. With Jonathan I first experienced the excitement of running aground on a falling tide, then having to climb out onto the mud and shove off. The mud, in most places, was merely black and sticky, all right when you had a sailing dinghy's transom to hang onto, and when you kept your feet moving fast, so that you didn't remain too long in one spot and sink in above your knees. But it could be perilous; several boys were lost in the Portchester mud while we lived there.

The small Portchester sailing club held races on Wednesday evenings and Saturday afternoons in the season. The club's honorary secretary and prime mover was our near neighbor Commander C.E. Hamond, D.S.O., D.S.C., R.N. retired—a smallish man with a neat van Dyck beard and a guernsey sweater that was usually flecked with sawdust. The sailing dinghies the Commander built in his garden workshop were of his own design, the Portchester Duck class, pram-bowed clinker boats with a short mast well forward and a single dipping-lug rigged sail. These craft naturally had such names as

*Teal, Merganser, Shoveller,* and *Goldeneye,* and their broad shallow hulls gave them a remarkably ducklike appearance and motion under sail, with a rippling bow-wave thrust out broadly on either side by their flat entries. The commander's newest boat, *Surf Scoter,* which he built for himself, did not help what we junior members of the club regarded as his short temper; she proved slower than the earlier boats in the class. The Commander blamed the heavier postwar timber he had been forced to use for her planking.

The Ducks were the jewels of the club fleet, forming a racing class of their own. But a motley collection of other craft sailed in the handicap class, went on independent voyages, or sat on their moorings, neglected or cherished by owners who sometimes just enjoyed sitting in them and tinkering with items of gear. It was difficult to live in Castle Street without owning a boat, whether you were naval officer, business man, or local waterfront type like Archie Paye and George Dore, who wore thigh boots and faded blue oiled-wool sweaters, went fishing in summer and wildfowling in winter, and spoke with accents of the sort that farming and fishing people seem to preserve almost deliberately in spite of the tendencies in modern life to iron out such traits. It wasn't difficult, therefore, to talk my father into buying a boat soon after we moved back to Portchester. It was a homely, solid thirteen-footer which was christened, at my suggestion, *Caprice.* I liked the sound of the word and hoped that it would enliven—perhaps even lighten—the sedate vessel. My father, realizing that I possibly knew more about sailing that he did, nicely allowed the roles prescribed by age and relationship to be reversed; he let me show him what Jonathan had showed me. In several races he crewed while I took the helm—a pattern that I now notice that friends of mine who are fathers also fall into with sons who imagine themselves more expert sailors, presumably in the hope that they are encouraging their heir's leadership qualities and nautical prowess, if not simply being paternally generous to them. And when *Caprice,* despite her name, began to seem like a clunker, my father supported my urgent desire to have a boat of my own. He loaned me £15 to buy the materials—I intended to build it myself.

The boat was a ten-foot-six-inch racing dinghy, designed for easy construction by young people, and sponsored by a yachting magazine; it was called the Cadet. I bought plans. I bought timber. I staked out a building site on a concreted section of the backyard behind the cottages, remembering to measure the doorways through to the street to ensure that the finished boat would go through. (I was a little less careful in seeing that the site was absolutely level; the boat, when completed, seen from fore or aft, had a very slight twist.) Most useful of all, I got a friend to help me with the construction.

Commander Hamond once asked me why I preferred to sail by myself; he felt sailing was a social activity, meant to benefit as many as a boat could reasonably hold. My idea—that sailing was a sublime pleasure most enjoyed on one's own—was quite unacceptable to him. "You're not a very public-spirited young man," he said gruffly on an occasion when I declined his suggestion that I take someone else along in *Caprice* as crew in a handicap race. (Apart from being happier by myself, there was a practical advantage that day, with very light airs, in sailing with as little weight in the boat as possible.) But the hard work of building a boat was clearly going to be easier and more fun with another pair of hands. Perhaps my motives weren't Machiavellian. My friend Howard Williams, nicknamed Wheezy because of his out-of-breath way of talking, wanted to help. He had a wry sense of humor and greater scientific skills than I. He wasn't much interested in sailing but enjoyed, as I did, seeing the skeleton of the boat come into being—the plywood gussets firmly holding together the corners of the transverse frames where these met at the chine; the keelson lying over the keel plank, providing on each side of this central member a long beveled edge to which the plywood bottom panels were fastened, making a tight joint; the mahogany transom sanded smooth and awaiting the varnish that would cause it to blossom in a shining skein, the lines running through the wood making it almost as alive as flesh.

The Cadet was the first of a dozen wooden boats that I was to build, rebuild, or restore. The knowledge of materials and structure that one gains in such a way seems to be an indispensable element not only of boat ownership but also boat handling—and something that someone buying a fiberglass boat direct from a dealer or factory may not have, lacking the knowledge a wooden boat builder acquires of what holds the whole thing together. This affects a boat owner's treatment of his craft, and his confidence in its behavior.

My infatuation with Cadet 326 was evident in the name with which I christened her: *Rhapsody*. She was painted a pale robin's-egg blue. The sails were a creamy Egyptian cotton, lovely to handle. She was light, and tremendously responsive compared with *Caprice* and the Ducks. My delight in possession wasn't reduced by finding out that, like most modern racing dinghies, she could be capsized. On the contrary, she could be capsized and easily brought up again by climbing over the windward gunwale and standing on the dagger board. (If one happened to be on the lee side when she went over, getting wet was inevitable; then one swam out from under the mainsail and round the stern to haul oneself up on the dagger board, pulling the boat upright in the process.) The side decks on which helmsman and crew sat were broad, and she took in very little water when lying on her side.

For two seasons I raced *Rhapsody* in club races and local regattas. When racing under Cadet class rules I had to have a crew, and I generally picked a youth who was younger and lighter than myself to adjust the jib sheet and dagger board and to hike out to windward when we were beating, keeping the boat as flat and upright in the water as possible. To get the fastest friction-free surface on the bottom that I could, I experimented first with floor wax and then black stove polish—which George Dore hinted had been banned as a "go-fast" aid at the turn of the century but remained highly effective. My reputation as an eager young sailor brought offers of crewing jobs on larger craft: on the ten-ton cruising sloop *Blue Jay,* belonging to Selwyn Slater, a button manufacturer who lived in a big house just west of the Castle; on the Dragon-class yacht *Valhalla,* chartered for Cowes week by Dr. Reginald Bennett, our local Member for Parliament; and on a brand-new long-distance cruising boat that a friend of some friends of my parents asked me to help sail on its maiden voyage down Channel. None of these ventures displayed me in a heroic light.

Selwyn Slater gave me the helm of *Blue Jay* one evening as we sailed up Portchester Creek, homeward bound. She drew six feet; the tide was falling. Mr. Slater said, "Keep her on a straight course," and went below to join his wife in the saloon with a gin and tonic. I steered as straight as I could, knowing that the tall pilings I could see marked the edge of the channel but—with my dinghy-racing instinct—edged over toward those on the port hand in order to cheat the ebb current. *Blue Jay* suddenly put her head down and came noisily to a halt. The tide gurgled past. Mr. Slater appeared in the hatch, took a surly look at the surroundings, and fired up the engine; grinding in reverse, it failed to budge the boat. Leaving me in the rapidly inclining cockpit, he handed Mrs. Slater down into the dinghy that we had been towing and proceeded to row her up the creek in the growing darkness; he would be back, he said, in four hours' time, when the tide, having turned, would be on the point of floating *Blue Jay* off again.

With Reggie Bennett I found myself in a new role—that of crew for a racing skipper at least as keen as myself. In fact, I shared the crewing duties on *Valhalla* during Cowes Week with Bennett's petite and pretty wife. We lived aboard their big old converted Brixham trawler, and raced daily in the tidal maelstrom of the Solent. The competition was hot—Dragons were a fashionable class at the time—and our opponents included the Duke of Edinburgh, advised by the veteran racing yachtsman Uffa Fox, in the royal yacht *Bluebottle*. I was unused to genoa jibs, spinnakers, sheet winches, and the language of a racing skipper in extremis. Coming round South East Middle buoy, swirling water, lurching yacht, the spinnaker dropping too fast in the water, the jib halyard jamming halfway up, *Bluebottle* on our weather quarter and overtaking, Mrs. Bennett looking salt-stained and beautiful as she attempted to haul aboard the sodden sail, and Reggie bombasting in a House of Commons voice that seemed to carry from one shore of the Solent to the other, shouting at me, snarled in a mass of line, "For God's sake get it sorted out, you ass!" Tears came to my eyes. Back on our mooring, Reggie uncapped a brown bottle and handed it to me. I put my lips to the bittersweet brown froth and sipped the ale, which I was unused to but manfully decided I would acquire a taste for. And as Reggie fastened the ties of the mainsail cover, Mrs. B. whispered to me, "It's only when racing, you know..." Presumably the good doctor didn't usually talk to his constituents or patients in that impatient way.

The oceangoing yacht, ketch-rigged, had just been launched from Thorneycroft's yard in Southampton. I was impressed by the rungs, fixed at intervals to the mainmast, that would enable the owner to go aloft to sort out jammed halyards and loose fittings. He intended to cruise single-handed in the Arctic—possibly to get as far away as he could from fleets of racing boats charging violently around the Solent. I had been asked to crew for him on the maiden, shakedown trip to Falmouth, and I was looking forward to my first sail down Channel. Unfortunately, when we set out, the wind was blowing hard against the tide where the Solent squeezes past Hurst Point. As the yacht charged up and down the steep ridges, I saw what the chart meant by the warning "Overfalls." Here a bottle of sweet vermouth fell out of a beautifully carpentered cupboard and smashed on the cabin sole. As I picked up the shards of green glass and mopped up blood-red liquid I became suddenly over-aware of the elegant woodwork—in this case, the strips of holly inlaid between the teak floorboards. I became dizzy with impending disaster. I headed swiftly for the cockpit and the lee rail. In a little while, after the owner had kindly given me the helm, hoping it would distract me from my seasickness, and I was having trouble concentrating on the course, he said, "You know, I think we'd better drop into Poole harbor so that you can get a train home."

*Rhapsody*'s slight kink didn't affect her speed. I won many races in her. Prizes included a clasp knife, book tokens, and a pound note in a municipal envelope handed to me by a mayor's wife, which I added to a token and used for buying books about sailing. The pleasure of winning a race was as close as I'd ever got to feeling total joy: the sensation of pride dovetailed with well-being suffused every part of me, surging through nerves and tissue that had been deliciously drained by suspense and exertion. The actual act of winning seemed a marvelous bonus after the pleasures of sailing. There were moments when my identification with the boat and its motion was just about complete—when the sails were precisely set for the course and the strength of the wind; when two fingers on the tiller provided the exact touch on the helm, the barest nudge being all that was needed to change direction without making the rudder brake the boat; and when the dagger board vibrated with an almost elemental strumming—the tune being one that let me know everything was as right as it could be and *Rhapsody* was moving as fast as ten and a half feet of Cadet dinghy ever could. There were other, quieter times, equally exciting in their way, when the surface of the water would be streaked by faint cat's-paws and the art was to make the dinghy ghost along. I sat absolutely still, listening to my heart beat, pretending not to notice the other boats close at hand but in fact conscious of what they were doing. There is a narcosis of the depths that affects the judgment of divers; this was a rapture of the surface that pervaded every sense and heightened the interplay of instinct and decision.

Of course, these rapturous occasions didn't always culminate in first prizes. The Portsmouth Harbour Cadet championship was held one summer at the Hardway Sailing Club, at a place near Gosport where an ancient hard or slipway gave access to the water—the name's more obvious connotation didn't register until later. Twelve boats were entered; it was light airs; and I made a bad start—I was over the line a fraction of a second before the gun and had to come back and restart. However, on the first leg I made up the lost ground. On the second leg I developed a long lead over the rest of the fleet. The third, penultimate leg took us up Fareham Creek, and as we began it I didn't see how I could lose the race if I kept things going the way they were. Along the middle of the channel was moored a close-packed procession of mothballed naval ships—destroyers, frigates, fleet auxiliary tankers. The most direct course to the next mark took me just to starboard of them, which was also on their lee side. It was high water and the tide was slack. I didn't sail right alongside them, knowing there would be no wind under their high gray flanks, but I also didn't sail too far to leeward of them, not wanting to increase by too much the distance the boat had to sail. And there *Rhapsody* came to a stop. Clearly the wind took a greater leap over the warships than I had imagined possible. There were moments when a little breeze reached me, and *Rhapsody* ghosted forward a brief way. But this was just a tease, enough natural encouragement to keep me there, hoping the breeze would continue.

The rest of the fleet of Cadets saw my plight. They took a longer, semicircular, course across to the far edge of the creek, well clear of the windshadow of the moored ships. I watched them begin to move out that way. A tiny puff arrived, and *Rhapsody* went forward. I decided to hang on a little longer. The puff died. The other Cadets were abreast of me, beginning to go by. I put the helm hard over and began to make a slow escape at right angles to my previous course, heading across the creek. By then it was too late. On the last leg to the finishing line I caught one boat. I was next to last at the finish. It was one of those incidents—defeat snatched despite the open hands of victory—that are painful enough in themselves, but that also stick in the memory, seeming almost intimidatingly symbolic, as though they might prefigure the way life—if one didn't stay a hundred percent alert—could turn out.

# 13

THE MOST PROMINENT FEATURE OF MOTHERS, AS SEEN by sons, is their capacity for worry. "I'm going sailing," I'd announce to my mother, deliberately keeping the information skimpy, but knowing that she would say, "Where are you sailing to?" and "When are you coming back?" I wasn't sure; and even if I had definite ideas about the destination and duration of the voyage I had in mind for the day, with a sparkling southeasterly and the ebb running out for the next three hours, I didn't want to divulge my plans. A measure of suspense was part of the pleasure of the adventure; and anyway, my goals might change en route. And so I would dash out, saying cheerfully, "See you later on"—knowing that she would worry on and off until I returned that evening after a wonderful sail by myself to the Isle of Wight in *Shoveller,* hauling the Duck up on Seaview beach for half an hour while I lunched off an ice cream, and then sailing back again. Perhaps she would have worried more if I'd told her what I had in mind.

The worry was generally counterproductive as far as my mother was concerned. Her giving expression to it made me shrink away from it, and made her persist, made her go on fussing, as it appeared to me, and made me become all the colder and less amenable to whatever it was she was giving as the reason for her anxiety. It was hard for her to enter a room where I was working, bringing me, say, a cup of coffee and a biscuit, without making her presence felt beyond the moment of leaving;

so that as she departed she would say "Well, now I'll leave you to it" (meaning my work, giving a dramatic and unwelcome importance to the school essay I was writing, and leading it to seem to me therefore doubly insignificant). And a few steps further on she would turn back to ask, "Did you want your door left open or shall I close it?"—to which I would reply, trying hard not to be curt, "It doesn't matter—either way." And the effect, which perhaps subconsciously she intended, was to prolong her visit to me, to sustain her motherly solicitude in the atmosphere or in my brain, vibrating as it was with suppressed irritation as I tried to recall what I'd been writing about Palmerston's foreign policy. Quite often I felt I couldn't stand it a minute longer—it was suffocating! And yet I recognized that it was love that lay behind it. Once or twice I reminded myself that she had been deprived of her son for more than four years, and perhaps she was making up for the loss. (Years later, my mother looked out on a September day from her dining-room window across the New Forest and remarked, with what struck me as fellow feeling, "The mares are on their own now. Last week all their little foals were taken from them.") But any good intentions that I silently pledged in this respect were easily forsworn. My sulky taciturnity drove my mother to feats of psychic reconnaissance. She asked questions that were—transparently—probes. She could read my mind. And this led me deliberately to change my mind so that—by the time of my reply—she was wrong in her assumption and I could deny it. With a fond smile she would say, "You must be tired"—and I would spurn the sympathy, the maternal care, the intrusion on my inner self. "No, I'm not," I'd reply, smothering a yawn. The closeness was threatening to overwhelm me and I would fight it.

At the time, in the thick of things, I didn't give credit

to various other unspoken and less aggravating expressions of maternal concern: apple crumble; beef casserole with dumplings; ironed shirts and darned socks. The ability of children to take their parents for granted is something that doesn't change a great deal from generation to generation, and I was no exception. I found it easy to slip into an attitude of slightly scoffing superiority toward my mother—humoring her whims and laughing at expressions that were traditional and even involuntary with her (such as "If a job's worth doing, it's worth doing well," or "If at first you don't succeed, try, try, and try again"). The laughter did not prevent these sayings from having profound effects; presumably she had been saying them from my early childhood; and now, though God forbid that I should actually say them myself (except perhaps to my children in the disarming, quoted form of "My mother always used to say, 'If a job's worth doing . . . ,'" etc.), I have to acknowledge that "deep down," in that part of me where lie buried the tune of "The Teddy Bears' Picnic" and the words of nursery rhymes like "Wee Willie Winkie," I believe in the truth of what she was saying. An apple a day. If at first you don't succeed you should keep trying until you do. And when I married, I was not very surprised when, on our honeymoon, my darling wife retreated a few steps down some hotel stairs, down which she saw me advancing. "I know," I said, as she was on the point of explaining, "it's bad luck."

My father resisted my mother's worries with consistent good humor—although he sometimes worried quietly about her. Yet his manner occasionally made it seem as if he didn't take her seriously, and sometimes, when she would have referred once again to what she had given up in order to marry him, i.e., her responsible job at the American consulate in Southampton, perhaps alluding by the way to important people she had met in those years, to the number of secretaries she had been in charge of, to her work in regard to Russian refugees who had been trying to gain admission to the United States, and to fancy dinners she had gone to on great ocean liners, like the *Lusitania* or *Leviathan;* and when my father, in response to such references, would have said, with a laugh, "If you had stuck with your job I would have been saved from however many years it is of marriage and washing up"—sometimes, then, she would get a little cross. "You don't know how jolly lucky you've been, my boy," she'd say. (My father now and then called her "my dear girl," which at the time I thought soppy but now think was pretty sweet.) On only one occasion did I hear her threaten to walk out of the house—and I think she did walk out, for half an hour or so, while my father tried hard not to look very worried indeed as he went on preparing supper in the Dovercot kitchen.

This may have been at the time when she had just learned to drive. She had taken lessons with a driving instructor and, to my father's amazement, passed the driving test at the first attempt. My father could not bring himself to let her use the car, at that point a rather elegant if elderly 1938 Riley. My mother, although cross, must have felt that to some degree his fears were justified—that her passing at first attempt was a complete fluke, and that she was altogether too nervous a person to be in sole charge of a motor vehicle. She let herself be persuaded that my father's estimation of her driving ability was more accurate than that of the Department of Road Transport's inspector, but she was also naturally furious that she allowed herself to give in. It seems to me now, from this distance, that my father—in making her thus dependent on him—made himself indispensable to her. Certainly there was never an instant's suspicion as far as I was concerned that the Bailey family was ever threatened by serious tremors, by sundering and disruption of the sort that has become familiar to many households in recent years. Perhaps my father's jocular response to my mother's worries was his way of releasing some of the pressure that builds up within a relationship that is regarded by both partners as made for life.

They shared—and still do—an interest in many of the local institutions that do good and serve as social cement. My father kept the accounts for the Portchester branch of the British Legion. My mother rolled bandages for the Red Cross and collected donations for the Cheshire Homes for the disabled. On a less formal basis their good works included simply remembering to make an extra dish of dessert, say a trifle, and taking it at dinner time to an elderly lady who lived on her own across the street, or saving a Sunday newspaper to pass on to an old man in reduced circumstances. My mother, having befriended someone, remained in touch with them thereafter; she continued to write to Portchester neighbors long after she and my father had been moved on by the bank.

One of her correspondents was Blanche Talmash, a woman who had cleaned at Dovercot several mornings a week. My mother never failed to send a small money order to her every Christmas, and would get in return a thankful if curiously punctuated letter giving news of the Portchester weather and the redevelopment at the top end of Castle Street— "Fish shop has closed down and two cottages empty, wont know Portchester like it used to be, theres only the Red Lion and the Railway Hotel standing on that side of the road, how do you like these dark mornings..." Mrs. Talmash lived in a small council house; she had—at least in my memory—never-ending difficulties with her family and a constant cold, which didn't prevent her from exuding a resilient good cheer as she talked of how her son-in-law had lost his job and the grandchild had gland problems and her husband was having trouble with the Social Security about his sick benefits from the last time he was off work. Flicking a mop, pushing a Hoover, sprinkling Harpic disinfectant in the loo, and polishing the brass where it showed, she managed to give our house a tidy appearance, no less real for being superficial. She was one of those "gems" that the social structure allowed to persist for the benefit of better-off households; and charring provided her with a moneymaking occupation and a national insurance stamp in a world restricted for her by lack of education and of other employment opportunities. My mother was grateful to her, and Mrs. Talmash remained grateful to my parents. She ended one letter: "Let me Wish you both a Very Happy and Prosperous New Year as you both deserve."

My father, when it came to it, was less apprehensive about my learning to drive. He took me out himself and showed me the workings of choke and accelerator, gears and clutch. Some Saturday afternoons we combined a lesson with attendance at a football match—driving to the United Services ground in Portsmouth to watch rugby, or to Fratton Park to watch soccer. Portsmouth, nicknamed Pompey, who since then have spent several decades scrambling around in the third and fourth divisions of English association football, were then one of the leading teams in the first division; in 1949 and 1950 they won the league championship. The crowds that filled the Fratton Park terraces gave vent from time to time to a powerfully encouraging chant known as the "Pompey chimes." Among the footballers I admired were Tom Finney of Preston North End; Tommy Lawton, center-forward of Notts County; Frank Swift, the goalkeeper of Manchester City; and Stanley Matthews, the Blackpool wing-forward, who could dribble the ball around the most stalwart defenders. Football shorts were long and baggy, and goalies usually wore cloth caps. The Portsmouth team's great strength was its rugged half-back line of Scoular, Frewin, and Dickinson; and perhaps the greatest of these was left-half Jimmy Dickinson, who often played for England. I wasn't much good at soccer when we played it at school, but possibly because of this I took the greatest delight in watching Dickinson making a tackle, the other player seeming to come to a shuddering halt as he met the wall of Dickinson's boots and calves, and the ball coming out of this collision firmly under Dickinson's control, tapped sideways a few paces, brought forward into a gap, then shot a long way into the other half to a waiting teammate.

The gap between my father and me, created by the war years, was partly bridged by these occasions. Even so, it took me a long time to get to know him and realize that things weren't as open-and-shut with him as one assumed. He seemed, at first glance, to share most of the racial intolerance of British people sheltered from contact with those of different-colored skins, but when in time he met—through the gradual spread of family entanglements—persons who were light or dark brown rather than pink in hue, it didn't seem to matter. (Perhaps the fact that by then many of the finer athletes, footballers and cricketers in Britain were of West Indian blood may have eased him this way.) Moreover, although without obvious "artistic" interests, a man never to be found in galleries or museums, he liked drawing, and he made precise, sensitive sketches of women's heads and bowls of flowers. Of quite powerful physique, he was rarely aroused to anger (the incompetence of other professional people, generally solicitors and insurance men, was about the only thing to get him fired up), and although he was nervous with dogs, birds particularly seemed to find him sympathetic, sparrows coming to the back door to eat out of his hand and robins, once fed, following him around the house. He was the sort of fisherman who threw back the few fish he caught.

# 14

It seems curious to me now that I didn't make frequent comparisons between my parents and the Spaeths, but nor had I done so while in Dayton. What was in the foreground in one place bulked large, and didn't strike me as having much to do with what was in the other. Now, I can remember that Eloise was glamorous, Otto forceful; my mother was pretty, my father handsome. But at the time I didn't make these comparative judgments, just as I didn't when we lived in Castle Street think, say in regard to pictures and books, that the Spaeths had had a lot of them and we had few. Many of the books at Dovercot had been bought by my parents as special offers advertised in the *Sunday Express,* sturdily but cheaply bound sets of the works of Dickens and other notable nineteenth-century novelists: *Jane Eyre, Pride and Prejudice, The Woman in White, The Mill on the Floss.* Their crimson bindings, packed into the shelves of a narrow, dark-stained bookcase that stood, sentrylike, in one corner of the dining room, produced the impression of a warm but impenetrable mass. You needed to put two fingers firmly on top of the compressed pages in order to pull a volume out. But books, even if not owned in profusion, had to be treated with care: that doctrine was instilled in me from an early age as my mother, quoting Roy Bower, told me that books should never be put down with their spine uppermost and their pages spread apart; moreover, you should never turn the pages with gloves on. *I* cared for books—in books that I acquired as presents or prizes I stuck one of the bookplates that

I'd brought home from Dayton, a gauzy label saying "This book belongs to Tony Bailey," decorated with the head of a silly-looking spaniel. This was later replaced, courtesy of the Golden Hour organization, by another bookplate showing an owl sitting on a pile of ancient volumes, one of which was opened to reveal the words Ex Libris. A blank space below the illustration gave room for me to write my name, generally as A. C. Bailey. So, if I now peek into books from this stage of my life, say *The Golden Warrior* by Hope Muntz or *Racing Dinghy Handling* by Ian Proctor, I am greeted by a long-eared dog looking like Charles II or an owl staring crossly somewhere over my right shoulder. At 630 Runnymede there had been a library-cum-card room downstairs, and upstairs, on a wide landing overlooking the front garden, an alcove where I was sometimes made to take afternoon naps. Here there were shelves inset into a wall over the couch, containing among other volumes Melville's *Moby Dick* and Stefan Zweig's *Beware of Pity.* Also impressive to me because of their size were *The Story of the Irish People* by Seamus Macmanus, testifying to Eloise (O'Mara) Spaeth's ancestral heritage, and a hefty Bible, printed in Gothic German characters, that bore witness to Otto's.

My own reading—begun, according to my not-unbiased mother, with a regular perusal of the *Daily Telegraph* at the age of three—passed through stages marked by loyalty to the *Dandy* and *Beano* comics; to Batman and Captain Marvel in America; to *Hotspur, Boy's Own,* and the *Meccano* magazine; and eventually to *The Navy* and to *Flight,* which had fascinating isometric cut-away drawings showing fuselage construction. Cartoon books describing the adventures of Rupert Bear were succeeded by more sparsely illustrated volumes about William, Richmal Crompton's naughty boy hero; Biggles, the intrepid airman; and Bulldog Drummond, secret agent. In my bedroom at Dovercot I installed my own shelves to accommodate books from Roy's New York book club, my sailing books, and books I received at school speech days: a popular history called *English Saga* by Arthur Bryant; a collection of essays entitled *Design in Modern Life;* and an account of the explorer, *Livingston's Last Journey.* A prize bookplate had already been put in place in these bearing the motto *Labor Omnia Vincit.* These worthy books, in fact, didn't do much to promote any ambitions I might have had to become an architect or explorer; they still seemed to be saying the solemn "well done" that had accompanied their presentation on the platform in front of the school. For a while I displayed some talent for art, and one Christmas present from a relative who had obviously asked "What shall I give him?" was a book called *How to Draw Sail and Sea,* one of a series of which I also acquired *Tanks and How to Draw Them* and *How to Draw Locomotives.* One of my favorite possessions was a Dutch school atlas from the 1880s containing not just maps but diagrams of sluices, drainage canals, and sea defenses. After poring over it for a while, I invented countries, particularly islands, drawing coasts and hills, towns and harbors.

One week I lay in bed with mumps, most of my features and vital parts sorely swollen. The curtains were pulled to keep out light regarded as possibly harmful to my vision. But I read anyway. I read John Buchan's *Wychwood* and after that his *Greenmantle.* I read aloud lines like "I may be sending you to your death, Hannay." I liked the outdoorsiness of Buchan's yarns, and wasn't put off by the ramshackle plots and the somewhat old-fashioned pontificating about the Empire and White Men—who were, it was understood, superior types. The Germans in *Greenmantle* presented Buchan with a problem, since although they were the Enemy they weren't

Kaffirs or Jews (whose whiteness was questionable). But Hannay works out a solution, which allowed the Germans to be White Men but also excessive types: "Then I realised something of the might of Germany. She produced good and bad, cads and gentlemen, but she could put a bit of the fanatic into them all." Buchan's books were nicely pitched for boys who weren't sure what girls were all about. There was much male camaraderie and male antagonism; women were uncomprehended or idealized. For instance—"Women had never come much my way," narrates Hannay. "I had never been in a motorcar with a lady before, and I felt like a fish on a dry sandbank."

The teacher at Price's responsible for alerting us to the rules of English grammar and the delights of literature was H. Ralph Thacker. He looked somewhat like Roy Bower, bespectacled, square of face, with a laugh that sometimes carried a swift message of sarcasm but was more often cheering, appreciative of a barely perceptible trace of promise in one of his flock. The best teachers—or best godfathers—are those who summon forth abilities we didn't know we had in us. To be valued warmly by Mr. Thacker's sharp gaze was to feel briefly a little better about the spotty, gray-flannel-clad lump of incipient manhood that was oneself. "Rather fantastic, but very well composed," wrote Thacker at the end of an early, pseudo-Hannay story of mine entitled "An Escape from a Concentration Camp in Siam." With Thacker we read poems in *The Poet's Tongue*—an anthology edited by W. H. Auden and John Garrett; we learned poems by heart, since this was part of Thacker's method. We stood up and recited stanzas of Hilaire Belloc's "Tarantella"—"Do you remember an inn, Miranda?"—or Gerard Manley Hopkins's "Wreck of the Deutschland," and I began to register feelings that corroborated what

Auden and Garrett claimed poetry to be—"memorable speech." It could be memorable even if you didn't really understand it.

Of course we had our own built-in ideas of poetry. There was a rhyme in circulation:

> One fine day in the middle of the night,
> Two dead boys got up to fight.
> Back to back they faced each other,
> Drew their swords and shot each other.
> A deaf policeman heard the noise,
> And came to kill the two dead boys.

The mysteries of paradox! There was military-inspired folk song:

> There were rats, rats, big as bleedin' cats,
> In the store, in the store,
> There were rats, rats, big as bleedin' cats
> In the quartermaster's store.
> My eyes are dim, I cannot see,
> I have not brought my specs with me,
> I—have—not—brought—my—specs—with—me.

So the influences were various. For Thacker, who told us to write for homework a poem entitled "London," I composed (aged thirteen):

> By the roar of busy streets,
> Wakened on a misty morn,
> Millions of people, young and old,
> Get up at break of dawn.
>
> The River Thames still flows by
> As off to work they go.
> Old London Bridge still spans it,
> As it has since long ago.

This went on for several bathetic stanzas, taking in the Houses of Parliament, Nelson's Column, and the Cenotaph. "First-rate," said Thacker, generously ignoring the limitations of my sightseeing tour of metropolitan high spots, the faulty history (London Bridge had been rebuilt several times since the construction of the one I had in mind), the echoes of the Seven Dwarfs' song from *Snow White* in line 6, and in the final stanza a good deal of pomp, circumstance, and sub-Churchillian rhetoric. This had come forth in a facile rush made evident by the increasingly rapid scrawl with which I penned the last lines with my black Waterman. "Not bad at all," said Thacker. "Now, for homework, memorize either Yeats's 'Sailing to Byzantium' or Roy Campbell's 'Horses on the Camargue.'" At home at this time I produced a few handwritten issues of a newspaper called *The Castle Street Courier*, whose hard news was mostly sailing and cricket results but included a report—concocted like everything else by me but attributed to "Our North American correspondent, T. Spaeth"—describing a Midwestern sighting of flying saucers.

To Thacker I attributed the "Distinction" grade I was awarded in the School Certificate Latin exam. "If you're doing Virgil," he said, "you might take a look at Homer." So I bought the chocolate-brown-and-white-backed Penguin translation of *The Odyssey* and read it; it seemed to me nearly as exciting as Buchan and Biggles; and somewhere in the exam I managed to make a comparison between Aeneas and Odysseus, showing that I knew (had actually read!) the seminal work. A little later I bought Yeats's *Collected Poems*. Perhaps recalling my mother's insistence that I was, through the Molonys, descended from Brian Boru, last of the Irish kings, I stood in my bedroom declaiming "Who Goes with Fergus?"—

> Who will go drive with Fergus now,
> And pierce the deep wood's woven shade
> And dance upon the level shore?
> Young man, lift up your russet brow,
> And lift your tender eyelids, maid,
> And brood on hopes and fear no more...

"Are you all right up there?" my mother called from the floor below.

"Quite all right, thanks," I said.

But not all my reading was at that exalted level. I sank into family sagas about fame and fortune, the pursuit of power and women; big, solid books like *The Crowthers of Bankdam* by Thomas Armstrong, *South Riding* by Winifred Holtby, and *Fame Is the Spur* by Richard Llewellyn; volumes that kept me turning the pages but also left me with a feeling of itchy dissatisfaction. These books came from Boots subscription library in Fareham. There was a period of several months, in fact, when my emotions were absolutely overwhelmed by a girl junior assistant in Boots library and my reading accelerated. I read prodigious quantities of books. And when my own demand for reading matter seemed insufficient for the purpose of getting me to the library often enough, I asked my parents if I could change their books for them. We had a Class B membership, which permitted us to take out any book except brand-new ones (these were reserved for Class A members paying a higher subscription).

I walked in to the front shop of Boots, given over to their main chemist's business, past the two facing counters where medicines were dispensed and soap and cosmetics were sold, hoping I wasn't going to blush brick-red as I ran this gauntlet; I was sure the salespeople apparently involved in transactions with men buying razor blades or mothers with coughing babies would notice me, and know my motives were more than literary. I plunged through the doorway into the library behind. The first thing to do was hand back the books I had brought, my heart plummeting if the girl I hoped to see wasn't on duty. How could I turn around at that point and leave, walk the streets of Fareham for an hour, and then come back in again, trusting she'd be there! My heart pounded just as much if she was there and taking not the slightest interest in me. She didn't realize she was the object of my raging passion, but calmly slipped the cord of an elderly lady's Class A reader's ticket through the grommeted hole in the base of the uniform library cloth binding of a new novel by Georgette Heyer. I dithered along the shelves of fiction, travel books, historical biographies. I took down Ernest Hemingway's *To Have and Have Not* and stood there pretending to peruse it, snatching a glance to where she was, now chatting with one of the other girls who worked with her. Were they, by adolescent chemistry, chatting louder, giggling more, because I was there? And when I had prolonged my presence in the library, in her presence, as long as I dared, I tried to pick the right moment when she wasn't waiting on anyone else, so she could deal with my selection of books. Then the books that I'd be reading in the next few days would be books that she had touched, that had to do with her. I'd say to her "Thank you very much" and "Good-bye" in a way that should convey to the least sensitive creature in the world the fact that I admired her. But, having dumped my books on the counter without looking at me, she was sticking the book cards that she had stamped in a little rack, against the day's date, and was already talking to her girlfriend again.

# 15

HER NAME WAS POPPY. FOR NO CLEAR REASON MOST OF the girls I knew in those years had the names of flowers. There had been Heather in Bursledon; there was to be Rose and, at a later date, Iris. I have since fathered four daughters and at no point felt a floral urge when it came to naming them—surely there is a danger that girls so christened will grow up to look not at all like the blooms they've been named after; or, conversely, that they will come to resemble their name flowers all too well. I remember Rose with rosy cheeks, Iris as tall and pale, and Heather as having freckles that amplified moorland associations already provoked by plaid skirts and Pringle sweaters— "jumpers," as they were called.

I began—as my visit to Boots library suggested—with terror enhanced by ignorance. Presumably some fortunate youths grew up with an instinctive appreciation of the fact that, in general, girls were as interested in boys as boys were in them. I did not. Even when the evidence for this was thrust in front of my nose, I found it hard to get outside my own desperate self-consciousness to see it clear. Peter Blewden and I usually rode home from school on a Southdown bus. We sat on top, and most of the time several Wykeham House girls were up there too, laughing, glancing around, calling attention to themselves although seeming to huddle together for mutual protection. Peter and I sat as near to them as we could; two, we knew, were Rose and Sarah. Under their hats—panama in summer, felt in winter—

their hair moved enticingly as they bent their heads together.

My encounters with Rosie (as Sarah called her) were limited to bus rides. We exchanged occasional snatches of banter. Anything resembling a direct smile from her set me up for days. Waiting to fall asleep, I imagined situations of the archetypal George, dragon, and princess sort where Rosie was in danger and I came to her aid. Such fantasies presumably have some basis in reality, despite feminist arguments that women can stand very nicely on their own feet without male help, thank you. Or is the reality that womankind like Rosie and Sarah can indeed be independent and men need to think they are important to the fair sex? Life to date has not resolved this question for me. Women seem to say at one moment that they desperately need you, and at the next to tell you to stop annoying them with your dominating presence.

Not that, then, I thought of Rosie in terms of womanhood. The women I knew well were mothers and aunts. However, the world apparently included other women—loose women, fast women, and women who "sold their bodies," though what that entailed remained unsure; prostitutes, we believed, could be identified by ankle bracelets or a band of cloth around one ankle as a badge of the trade (goodness knows where we got that idea from, or what trouble it may have caused women wearing surgical bandages around sprained ankles). And I was beginning to realize that older women—anything from eighteen upward—could arouse powerful sensations, of a different kind or a different voltage from those aroused by Rose and her contemporaries. The daughter of one of my mother's friends was an art student in London; she looked, I thought, very much like the actress Jean Simmons, whom, pert and pretty, I had recently seen going mad in Laurence Olivier's *Hamlet.* But although she took an interest in my drawing, from her point of view the four or five years difference in our ages made me just a boy, and she gave no hint of recognizing that she had an effect on me. However, among the local businessmen my father got to know through the bank was one who occasionally came to our house for a drink, bringing his wife. Once or twice, watching Mrs. W. as she toyed with a glass of sherry, I met her eyes; there was a momentary flash, a slight parting of the lips that might be a private smile. I wondered if the gooseflesh on the back of my neck was highly visible. Sometimes Mrs. W. came into my thoughts unbidden—her well-tailored suits, her smooth blond hair. A year or so later I read Stendhal's *Le Rouge et Le Noir,* and Julien Sorel was recognizably a hero from whom I had much to learn. I wished that I had had the gumption to try to hold Mrs. W.'s hand, or, sitting next to her at the table having tea, had pressed my knee against hers as she took a delicate bite out of a cucumber sandwich—one of the contributions my father liked making to occasions where sandwiches were called for, meticulously arranging the contents inside the bread, and neatly cutting all the crusts off.

I did a number of things purely because they provided a way of meeting girls. I joined the local branch of the Young Conservatives for that purpose. Labour continued to govern the nation, but I was less interested in promoting the downfall of Mr. Attlee than in attending events organized by the young Tories for the entertainment of Portchester youth. These events included Saturday-night "socials" at the Parish Hall, a drab, barnlike structure halfway up Castle Street where such functions as Women's Institute bring-and-buy sales and blood-donation drives were also held. Now and then there was a real band of three or four semiprofessional musicians, but generally a record player whirred out the music—first a Paul Jones to break the ice, a ring of boys circling a ring of girls, each taking as partner the person opposite when the music stopped; then a variety of dances, some traditional like the Veleta or Gay Gordons, some colloquial and comic like the Hokey-Cokey, Palais Glide, and Lambeth Walk, and some plain basics like the quickstep and waltz. I had been taught the rumba, samba, and foxtrot at Miss Botts's dancing school in Dayton, and though some of the knowledge had faded, certain tricks and skills—like hesitating and reversing—remained. Dancing was still at this point a matter of holding on to someone else; the pre-stereo music was not deafening. There was a definite delight in swinging around on the deal floorboards, more or less in the rhythm, sensing what your partner was doing.

Although physical contact between the sexes often seems as full of difficulty as of delight when one is young, there were for me early pleasures that can be recalled with a little of the tingle they produced at the time—holding hands with Iris Rutledge, for example. Iris—she must have been a year older than I—seemed very sophisticated. Iris had long cool fingers, and as I walked home with her from a social or from carol singing on Portsdown Hill, the calm, tactile message my fingers absorbed when intertwined with hers was one of blood-pumping excitement. A lot—and I had no idea how much—was implicitly to come.

I made no attempt to mix girls and boats. I took my sister, Bridget, sailing, but of course that wasn't the same thing. There was a higher importance attached to the sea, which was not to be sullied by association with Desire and Young Women. My mother must have seen this as one advantage of my addiction to sailing; her belief, often reuttered, was "Until you are a good deal older you ought to have lots of friends—don't go getting serious about just one too soon." I wouldn't have said there was much danger of that.

There was, in any event, a lot of hanging around attached to the business of girls—looking for them; waiting for them; hoping they would show up—all of which drained one's ardor for a while. There had to be better ways of spending one's time than worrying about creatures so remote and hard to make contact with. But the need to make that contact couldn't be denied. I went to Poole in Dorset for a schools' sailing championship; I didn't know anyone there. I stayed the night before in a small boardinghouse and after supper walked along the main street, looking in shop windows, thinking about girls, wondering if I would have the courage to speak to a girl if I encountered one, and what she would say. I walked the length of the street, almost to the edge of town, and back again. At one point a girl walked past on the other side, and, slightly relieved, I took it for an omen; that was where she was meant to be as far as I was concerned.

Finally I summoned the nerve to ask Poppy to go to a film with me. I hoped to find her alone in the library, but it never worked out that way. I wrote to her at the library—knowing this would draw down on me, on a future visit, the amused attention of her colleagues. But before she had the chance to answer, if that was what she meant to do, I decided to act ("Nothing venture, nothing win," was one of my mother's sayings.) I went to Fareham one evening and waited for her outside Boots. I turned my back on the shop entrance so that I wasn't too obvious to everyone on the staff and kept an eye open to the right, in the direction she would turn on her way to the bus station. And then there she was. She gave me a mischievous smile. I walked along with her. Would she like to come to the pictures with me in Portsmouth? She laughed. She said, "All right." I blurted forth suggestions of where we should meet and when, the following Saturday evening. Then I said, "Goodbye. I'm going to the bookshop." Which was a lie, but I couldn't stand being with her a moment longer.

I turned up at our appointed rendezvous at ten to six—a winter night. I was ten minutes early, but I didn't want her to get there ahead of time and think I wasn't coming. It was a row of bus stops at a place where various main roads came together, near Cosham: no shops, no houses. My intention was for us to get another bus from there to the cinema in Portsmouth. Apart from being dark, it was damp and foggy. Tall sodium street lamps turned everything a murky orange. Buses pulled up or went past, the heads of passengers apparent behind the misted-up windows. Occasionally one of them, like a goldfish nosing up to the inside of a bowl, would rub the glass and peer out to see where the bus had got to. The fog rolled in off the mudflats at the head of Portsmouth harbor and meshed with the coal smoke from the city's houses drifting north. I walked up and down to keep warm, looking at each bus as it approached—she had to be on this one. No. Then the next. No. I waited an hour. Had she forgotten—had she mistaken the time, the date? I didn't know her address or if she had a phone. At last I caught a bus home.

She had an excuse when I saw her next in the library.

"Sorry. My mum had a cold. I stayed in to look after her."

I believed her because there was nothing else to do. She said she'd meet me again the next Saturday. We met at the cinema—I couldn't stand the idea of the bus stop again, and thought it was a jinxed spot. Afterward we had coffee somewhere. She told me that she was just working in the library until there was an opening in the shop for a girl who wanted to become a chemist's dispenser. She wasn't really very fond of books.

# 16

"STILL IN SCARCE SUPPLY" WAS A PHRASE THAT NOW SEEMS to provide a wan keynote for those years. It wasn't until May 1950 that we could go into a restaurant and order a meal of more than three courses, costing more than five shillings. Meat was rationed well into the mid-1950s. But perhaps because any eating out that I did tended to be in tea shops, where pots of tea, scones, and rock cakes went on being sold to a stoical public, the stringencies of the time didn't have much impact on me. And whether I was too busy memorizing Yeats, or sailing *Rhapsody*, or fitfully pursuing Poppy, I didn't do much—if any—calm reflecting on the state of my country, whose pinstriped demob suit was beginning to look worn and shiny. The nation had ended the war with an accumulated debt of £3000 million; it had used up overseas investments of £1000 million by the close of the conflict, and exports were at a third of their prewar level. Despite the Marshall Plan, Britain had what Chancellor Hugh Dalton called "an apparently insoluble problem," with its gold and dollar reserves fast draining away. The foreign-travel allowance was completely suspended in 1948. The pound, that stooping form, was eventually devalued (from $4.03 to $2.80) in July 1949, acknowledging that it would never again be the vigorous runner (worth nearly $5) of prewar days. (For me, cashing ten dollars that Otto and Eloise sent me for Christmas, it meant more pounds.) But devaluation did increase exports; some Marshall Plan aid was used to purchase Virginia tobacco, believed vital to keep up the morale and production of British workers; and the country renounced any further assistance from the Plan a year before such help was due to end. Another keynote was the frequent government announcement of new production drives. It was claimed that one of the country's problems was a *shortage* of manpower: several million more workers were needed. The continued scarcity of just about everything was demonstrated by the fact that even in January 1947 soft drinks were unavailable under brand names and that in the streets of cities like Portsmouth the trams and trolleybuses had the roadways very much to themselves. When I took my driving test in Portsmouth at four o'clock one afternoon the difficulties were presented less by other motor vehicles than by hordes of workers, on foot and bicycle, who came pouring out of the dockyard gates.

It didn't occur to me that in Dr. Reginald Bennett, our member of parliament, I had a personal link with that great institution, whose slow rise to supreme influence in British government we traced in history lessons, and whose current legislative work we talked about in civics—had we known, we might have discussed it in terms of having reached its peak, losing ground once again to the ever growing and ever greater-spending executive machinery. Come to think of it, Dr. Bennett had been lucky to be chosen for the rock-firm Conservative seat of Fareham in 1945, when the general election produced such a massive nationwide swing to Labour, and many Labour supporters thought a new world had been ushered in. As far as I was concerned, Reggie Bennett was someone who wore a yachting cap, shouted a lot, and when living on his Brixham trawler served his guests crème de menthe cocktails from an apparently inexhaustible store of bottles of the sickly green fluid kept under the cabin sole. It might have helped my perceptions of government—or at any rate of the role of the opposition party—if he had invited me to visit the House of Commons as well as to crew for him at Cowes. Of course it was hard, reading newspapers, to avoid some of the drama pertaining to how the nation was run, and which the Tory papers often conveyed in demonological terms—thus Emanuel Shinwell incurred the blame for the 1947 fuel crisis; John Strachey, Minister of Food, was considered culpable for the disappearance of powdered eggs and the fiasco of the scheme to produce groundnuts in East Africa, which was meant to boost the native economy and provide Britain with cheap edible fats and oils; and Chancellor Stafford Cripps, stiff, hollow-cheeked, wasn't much pitied when he rode out one sterling panic and personal health crisis in a Swiss clinic. Cripps was also known as the man who had introduced potato rationing for the first time.

Along Portsdown hill—its green upper slopes cratered with white chalk quarries—postwar housing developments marched westward. They began with "prefabs," single-story flat-roofed boxes with steel-framed windows set in pastel-colored paneled walls; these were meant to last a few years until more substantial dwellings could be built, but some were still inhabited three decades later. The permanent structures that went up were not much of an improvement, either to look at or as a contribution to urban living. Long, look-alike streets of semidetached houses meandered along the hillside from Cosham to Paulsgrove (so named because of a tradition that the Apostle Paul had landed there), spoiling the hill while providing a fine view of the harbor for many of the occupants of the houses. Fortunately there was still plenty of grass on each side of the lane that climbed from Portchester to the top of the down, where I flew model gliders. Launched into the southwesterly breeze that was generally deflected up the escarpment, the glider would slide out and down for a moment before seeming to catch on the invisible lip of the wind, lift and sail far out before spiraling gently downward, giving me a long, bumpy run downhill to retrieve it. From the hilltop, where the obelisk commemorated Nelson within sight of the waters from which he had often sailed, I looked south to the mothballed warships, Portsmouth dockyard, and the spars of the *Victory*.

It was natural, living in Portchester, that I thought of going to sea. Naval officers lived all round us. The excitements and camaraderie of my voyage home on the *Ranee* were still sharply remembered. Although such books as *The Caine Mutiny* and *The Cruel Sea* were yet to appear, I had daydreams in which I stood on the bridge of a corvette or destroyer, wearing duffle coat, roll-neck sweater, and seaboots, and giving the man at the wheel quiet, precise orders—"Three points to starboard, Jones"—while enemy shells splashed around the ship and the captain lay, severely wounded, in his cabin. The First Lieutenant takes command. My father wrote for information about entry to the Royal Naval College at Dartmouth. Details were also acquired of the school at Pangbourne on the Thames where youths were trained for a career as officers in the Merchant Navy, though this didn't seem to me to have the glamour and possibility of rising to great rank in the Royal Navy—captain of a flagship; First Sea Lord.

And then voices of caution, even dissuasion, were heard. Several of the local naval officers, who had reached the rank of lieutenant-commander and then been retired involuntarily, pointed out the disadvantages of being thus axed, put on the beach in one's thirties or early forties and forced to lead a different life—less money, an uncertain future, having to take up chicken farming or selling insurance. Commander Hamond was happy building boats but would have been happier still in the service. One or two of the serving officers talked about the difficulties of leading a regular home life while having to put in long periods at sea. "You don't see much of your wife and family. Nothing you'd appreciate now, but later on, believe me..." Moreover, the empire was fading; the navy was shrinking; no war was imminent that would need battleships—or even all the cruisers and corvettes we'd got. Hence the mothballed fleet. Hence the warships that weekly went to the breakers. The message was, If I liked the sea and sailing, I was likely to enjoy them most by having a well-placed job in civvy street.

For that matter, did I really like the sea? I enjoyed sailing in the Solent. I loved beaches—sand and shingle, and the foam-flecked edge of the incoming tide. I liked the details of coasts and harbors, and took pleasure in the expertise I was slowly acquiring with small boats. But the sea? The sea, I remembered, was great gray rollers; was ships lurching, pitching, pounding. I recalled the Channel, wind against tide, beyond Hurst Point, and crouching at the lee rail as I turned inside out. Since then I've made a midwinter transatlantic passage on a small liner—arriving three days late due to storm conditions. I've been in a twenty-four-hour near-hurricane on the yacht race from Newport, Rhode Island, to Bermuda, when at one point the water inside our craft, an elderly forty-one-foot yawl, was up to the top of the cabin berths and the pump had clogged with soggy labels washed off cans of food. And I have decided that I am at best an agricultural sailor, fond of creeks and bays and inlets—sheltered water—and happiest when rarely out of sight of land. And that I made a correct decision when I told my father that perhaps the navy wasn't for me.

There was never any suggestion that I join the bank—no serious suggestion, at any rate. My father on one occasion said with a laugh, "I don't suppose you'd want to go into the National Provincial, would you?" I replied, also with a laugh, "No, thanks." At one point, since the matter of how I was to make a living concerned him, and since he felt bound to propose alternative careers (even as he felt bound not to emulate *his* father and impose a decision on me), we made a trip together to Southsea to talk with the senior partner of a firm of solicitors. I was given a somewhat repetitious rundown of the firm's activities, which were mostly in handling wills, estates, and house conveyancing. It was explained that I could be "articled" to the firm for a few years (which would cost my father some money) but that if I got on properly, made the right impression, and passed the right exams, I would end up as a fully qualified solicitor. When we came out my father looked at me for a reaction. Not seeing much of one, he said, "Something to think about, anyway."

When we walk together now in the New Forest, my father and I fall into step. One of us will change step to match strides with the other, so that our left feet and then our right feet go forward together. It may be partly the effect of army training on both of us; it may simply be an unconscious display of father-and-son affection. As we stroll along, we discuss mortgages, insurance, house repairs, how our cars are going—the daily matters of fact within which life moves, and which are interesting to both of us, even as they form means by which close feeling can be communicated. Much goes unspoken; some subjects might be too prickly. But sometimes one can be outspoken about the past in a way one can't about right now, when one feels the need to hoard certain matters privately, perhaps superstitiously, until they have matured—or disappeared. The other day my father and I were talking of legal matters, including what solicitors charge for their services. My father usually says—when the law is discussed—that solicitors have one of the best closed shops going, and he did so now: "It's all a big wangle, really—£400 for transferring the deeds of a house. I don't know how they get away with it."

I said, "Do you remember taking me to that firm of solicitors in Southsea?"

"Well, it is a comfortable profession." Some of my father's best friends were solicitors. "Good money for boring work. I suppose you could have done worse."

"My ambition then was to become a secret agent."

This was something that came about possibly as a result of listening to the radio adventures of Dick Barton and his pal Snowy and reading those of Richard Hannay and Bulldog Drummond. With a Christmas gift book token circa 1949 I bought *A Handbook for Spies,* an account by a man called Alexander Foote of various episodes in his life as a member of a Soviet spy network in Switzerland, working against Germany. In Foote's book I first read about Moscow Centre (this was long before Le Carré). Foote claimed to have been at first idealistically engaged by communism but gradually to have perceived the truth about Soviet *Realpolitik,* at which point he got out. I bought a Morse code outfit and, with Wheezy Williams several rooms away, sent messages back and forth. I invented cyphers and experimented with invisible inks. Sitting close to our dark brown bakelite Sobell radio in the dining room I switched to shortwave and tried to distinguish what I thought might be messages going to Moscow Centre from a Russian spy network in England. (I didn't know it but Klaus Fuchs was busily gathering British atomic secrets at that time. I also hadn't known it, but the recreation building known as the Playhouse on the Talbott Estate, across Runnymede Drive from the Spaeths' house in Dayton, had been used between 1944 and 1949 for work in developing atomic bombs—a radioactive element called polonium was processed there, used to trigger the bomb dropped on Nagasaki and later test bombs. All we knew as children in 1944 was that our play area on Talbott Hill had been restricted—"war work" was going on in the Playhouse. In the summer of 1947 it was still out of bounds behind a secure fence. In 1950 the heavily contaminated Playhouse was pulled down and seven feet of earth from under the foundations shipped away along with the cobblestones from the driveway.)

Eventually the apparatus of secret agentry seemed to me fusty and complicated—you needed to be better at math than I was to work out ciphers and codes. It was hard to imagine anyone being dippy enough to want to promote via those means world communism and Uncle Joe's Russia. Later, when reading about Maclean, Burgess, and Blunt, it struck me that adolescent fantasy and the need to have secrets, mixed with a dash of rebellious idealism, can be dangerous if it sticks. It seemed that our Morse code exercises had the greater effect on Wheezy. When I last heard from him he was doing his National Service with the Royal Signal Corps.

The Sobell, tuned to the Home Service, also brought into Dovercot news of the real world. In 1948 and 49 we heard of the deaths of Gandhi and Jan Masaryk; the Berlin airlift; dock strikes and a state of emergency in Britain; the end of sweet (i.e., candy) rationing; the escape of H.M.S. *Amethyst* under fire down the Yangtze River. The BBC, whether spreading enlightenment or making us laugh, was part of our household—a fact to which my mother bore frequent witness by the way she referred to the stars of radio and television; it was "old Gilbert Harding" and "old Richard Dimbleby," not because of their age but because they seemed like old friends. On one occasion Sam Costa, part of the team that made the comic radio series *Much Binding in the Marsh* (set on a fictitious airfield), came to open a fête in the Castle grounds. I photographed him as he got out of his car, his handlebar mustache suggestive of whirling propellers. Sam Costa's catchphrase on the program was "Good morning, sir—was there something?" (to be compared with that used by the cleaning lady character Mrs. Mopp, on the rival program *ITMA,* "Can I do you now, sir?").

There was, in that heavily rationed age, no shortage of idols or heroes—among mine were Winston Churchill and Fred Astaire. And, in articles and advertisements in the *Portsmouth Evening News,* which my father brought home after work, there was one area of interest to me that compared with today seems varied and spacious: new models of cars. A.C., Allard, Alvis, Armstrong-Siddley, Bristol, Humber, Hillman, Jowett, Lanchester, Lea Francis, Riley, Singer, Standard, and Wolseley were among them, to mention only those makes that are no more.

# 17

THE MAIN PORTSMOUTH-LONDON ROAD CLIMBS A STEEP hill as it goes north out of Petersfield, a Hampshire country town with a small equestrian statue of William III in the middle of the square, a weekly market, and a fine High Street terminating—just beyond a war memorial for the Hampshire Regiment—at the Red Lion Hotel. At the top of the London Road hill, on the right, a collection of gray Victorian buildings sits back from the road, with a clock tower and a signboard announcing that this is Churcher's College. I have driven by several times in the last thirty years without calling in. Churcher's rooms, corridors, staircases, hall, and grounds are fixed in my mind the way a theater might be for an actor who played in it over a testing two-year run of repertory productions and for whom recollection remains a trifle touchy, the images of certain physical or structural forms bringing along with them memory of high and low moments, the applause and the catcalls.

Even before Dartmouth loomed as a possibility, my parents had talked of sending me away to school. They were prompted by a feeling that is still widespread in upper and middle class Britain, that a boarding school, particularly of the public or "independent" sort, puts backbone into a youth while giving him a better chance in life—it was a way of ensuring him a slightly more secure niche in the system. The education he got was also fairly certain to be competent, if not superior. My parents couldn't afford to send me to a major public school, and I was fifteen before any move from Price's became a financial possibility for them. They looked at schools that local education authorities helped support, where tuition was free and only the boarding charges had to be paid for. Churcher's was one such school. It called itself a grammar school with a public school organization and had been founded by Richard Churcher, an East India Company merchant, in 1722. The school's crest showed an East Indiaman under sail. In 1948, the year I "sat" my school certificate exams at Price's, my father took me to Petersfield for an interview with the headmaster of Churcher's. It was agreed that I would start in the autumn term in the lower sixth form.

Start was the right word. I was a newcomer arriving in a place where most of the denizens had been for some years. Although this wasn't a new thing for me, the difference this time was that, being a boarder, there was no escape at the end of the school day—no home to go back to in the afternoon. My bedroom was a dormitory shared with twenty other boys. I took a partial refuge in my background; the nickname "Yank" resurfaced. It was a sort of camouflage, an idiosyncratic identity that stood alongside me as a foil or double, which took some of the attention and heat off me. And heat there also was. My arrival at Churcher's coincided with the onset of a physiological phenomenon—I couldn't stop myself from blushing. It was, I suppose, a manifestation of vehement self-consciousness, a demonstration of embarrassment that was intensified by the very act of going red in the face—like sending up a flare to draw attention. (And which presumably arose from mixed and contradictory impulses, the fear of being noticed and the desire to be noticed.) I blushed in hall during morning assembly. I blushed when sitting at the long tables in the dining room. I didn't have to be the subject of notice when it began to happen—I didn't need to be talking to anyone or be answering a teacher's question. In fact, action, or talking, sometimes prevented it—or so it seemed in my desperate search for methods to stop a blush occurring ( "Maybe if I start talking now it won't happen"). Things reached a point where if I wasn't blushing I wondered why I wasn't, and inevitably began to blush at that moment. I could feel the skin go hot on the back of my neck, on the sides of my face, and join in a glowing band across my forehead. My ears, burning red, were like a car's signal indicators both on at once. I felt sure people were thinking about me—were aware of what was going on in my mind and could read my thoughts—and *that* was embarrassing. I felt that I was the only person in the school so handicapped—that everyone else was filled with confidence. In the throes of extreme self-concern, I failed to apprehend that there were plenty of occasions in the course of a school day when others wished the ground would open and swallow them up.

Of course, much of the time my fellow pupils didn't notice me. Perhaps what felt like a vivid blush to me, inside it, seemed no more than a warm, healthy flush to spectators, not that different from the way a boy might look who had just come in from the sports field. Yet at other times they did notice—I sensed looks of amused appraisal, elbows nudging neighbors to glance at me. Sometimes someone would say—and it sounded very loud— "You've gone red, Yank," as if it were a thing I ought to know about, too.

Soon after coming back from Dayton I had several times walked in my sleep. One night at Park Gate my mother found me standing in my bedroom, eyes closed, waving one of the spearlike carved paddles Granddad Molony had brought back from the Gold Coast. Once at Dovercot I woke up (or thought I did) and had the sensation of being above my body, floating over it. Would I be able to get back into it? Somehow, though the process didn't form part of the action illustrated in my mind,

I did. One night at Churcher's I went to bed as usual in the dormitory, put my head down on the pillow at lights out with relief, and was soon asleep. When I woke up, it was with a start of absolute terror. I was standing in a darkened hallway—I had no idea where. Was it a dream, the worst nightmare ever? For a moment I was overwhelmed with all the fear of the dark that one has as a small child. A dim light seemed to come from around a corner; the walls gave off a faint, eerie gleam. I made out a window, with a curtain slightly stirring. I moved—I had to move; the fear of not doing so exceeded the fear that had kept me transfixed. I found a light switch. The hallway was in a part of the school, in the masters' wing, where I had never been before. I cautiously followed the carpeting round the corner and found a corridor that led back to what I recognized as my own part of the school, to my dormitory, and bed.

Early on at Churcher's I was sent with a group of other boys to be an extra in the film *The Happiest Days of Your Life,* some of which was being shot at Bedales, a coeducational school not far away. We were told to rush around the edge of a swimming pool; some had the extra pleasure of falling in. The stars of the film—who disappointingly were not on hand—were Margaret Rutherford and Alistair Sim. They weren't the happiest days of my life, those first few terms at Churcher's, but nor were they the worst, as it turned out. I occasionally wonder which actors of the time I would cast in the roles of my teachers—Alistair Sim and Alec Guinness would do well, perhaps in multiple parts. Teaching apparently involves a lot of acting—projecting one's personality; or does it seem that way to the student in the audience as he becomes familiar with the teacher's favorite rhetorical devices, his tricks of gesture, his physical characteristics and eccentricities, highlit by proximity and frequency of appearance on the classroom stage? I remember such features as the scrubby mustache of Mr. Kershaw, the English master who also produced school plays and edited *The Churcherian;* the stoop of hunchbacked Mr. Ives, the Latin master and librarian, his head permanently bent forward so that to look at you he had to twist it sideways, bringing his eyes nearly one above the other; the impish tone of Mr. Lane, who taught history and was the college organist and organizer of musical events; the tight little mustache and precise manner of Major Charles, who taught French and ran the Cadet Corps; the sly humor and—as it would now be called—camp manner of Mr. Turner, who was my form master and housemaster (though I didn't take geography, which was his subject); and the heavy-handed wit and growing bald patch of Mr. Schofield, the headmaster—all these exaggerated aspects of physiognomy and personality provided a rough-and-ready means of identifying them, and maligning them, but perhaps make it a little harder to discern the individuals who took lesson after lesson, marked countless essays, oversaw sessions of homework, delivered addresses of exhortation and rebuke, sat at the heads of dining tables, helped with games and clubs and societies, and got some of their pupils actually to "try harder," "concentrate more," "improve grip on grammar," and "achieve the success he is perfectly capable of."

Churcher's was a small school, with roughly two hundred day pupils and one hundred boarders, and about twenty on the teaching staff. The pupils were distributed in four "houses," named after British seafarers—Drake, Rodney, Nelson, and Grenville. All this made it easier for a late arrival like myself to get involved in the various activities meant to keep us busy and develop our talents. I served as orderly sergeant for the school Cadet Corps. I was secretary of the debating society and an assistant librarian. I helped edit the once-a-term magazine, *The Churcherian.* I sang in musical productions and acted in plays. In school, as I later found in the army, to be "keen" was the highest virtue, and for the moment I was keen to participate, keen to have a hand in the running of things that affected me, and keen not to be an outsider. Apart from being a new student I was special in that I was a Catholic—I didn't have to attend prayers but could sit in the corridor outside the swing doors to the assembly hall chatting quietly with the half dozen other declared adherents to loyalties other than Protestantism: several Jews, a few more Catholics, and—the real oddity—the dutiful son of vociferously atheist parents. I wouldn't have minded my special-category status if I had been a committed Catholic. But it seemed to me a bit of a sham, ducking out of school prayers for the sake of a religion I no longer felt bound to (going to Mass was really a matter of pleasing my mother). Moreover, the Bible that was used for reading out the morning lesson was the same work, in different translation, that Catholics used. The hymns being sung in assembly were addressed to the same God—and seemed to me better as music than those rendered by syrupy, predominantly female choirs in Catholic churches. So I defected; perhaps, too, I was seeking the anonymous comforts of the majority. I took my turn among the other sixth-formers in reading the lesson—and there was no anonymity in that, rather a brief minute or two in the limelight, in front of the school; I was making a determined counterattack on self-consciousness. I enjoyed raising my voice in hymn singing. I particularly liked John Bunyan's Puritan anthem, "He who would valiant be." I was at one with the hero who fought with giants, was beset with foes, but made good his right to be a pilgrim. When the doors opened after the service to let in the minority pupils to join the rest of the school in hearing the Head's announcements for the day, I gazed at them with condescension. They didn't know what they were missing.

At this point one trouble with thinking about those years is the difficulty of doing so without an upsurge of distaste for the adolescent one was, which may color the process of recollection unfairly. *That was me, and I couldn't help it.* Pimply. Shy, yet full of self-aggrandizing ambition. Incoherent yet wanting desperately to be articulate. Interested in various arts yet saturated with arrogant prejudices and philistine feelings. With an embarrassed shiver that the passage of thirty-four years does not alleviate I see myself on stage in Mr. Kershaw's production of *The Merchant of Venice,* on the verge of being flummoxed by absolute stage fright, and yet with the speeches of Antonio coming out of me as if from some sort of recalcitrant speaking machine. And it is hard not to applaud Mr. Kershaw's brilliant casting: I am as pompous and priggish as Antonio; Shakespeare makes him such a mealy-mouthed, self-regarding fellow. My rendering of the man is let down only by nervousness and hesitation; Antonio is nothing if not self-assured. Similarly, I recall speaking at a meeting of the school debating society against the resolution "This House would welcome a Tory victory in the general election." I declared that it was not the right time for the landowners to come to power—a somewhat anachronistic suggestion that presumably sprang from an essay I had been writing for Mr. Lane about Britain before the Reform Bill of 1832. I continued with the pronouncement that nationalization, a good thing, prevented monopolization, which was a social menace. When I stood up to speak and throw over any tenets of Young Conservatism still clinging to me, I was for a moment more aware of my audience—nine or ten partly attentive boys, one of whom was grinning—than I was of what I intended to say. In my head was a rushed muddle of thoughts. The words that began to tumble forth from my mouth were unsynchronized with the thoughts in my head. The sequence of ideas was all wrong. In my extreme self-concern I seemed to hear myself as I talked, the words echoing as they sometimes do on the transatlantic telephone. I could feel the rising red in my cheeks and ears and could see that two boys were now smirking at me and one wasn't listening at all. I was aware of too much. If only I could close out a great deal of that perception and just have logically ordered words coming from my lips! I could even look ahead to the vote that would take place in a few minutes and know that I would lose; the resolution would be carried. (It was.)

At the start of my third term—the summer term—I was made a prefect. This meant a partial co-option into authority, taking part (as the school rules put it) in the work of assisting the headmaster and staff in the maintenance of good order and discipline. Although not permitted to inflict corporal punishment, I was allowed to punish an offender with an hour's detention after the day's classes. I was given the privilege of entry to the prefects' common room. This was a den at the foot of the main staircase, a dugout from which we sallied forth to the duties of school life and which formed a refuge between standtos, lulls, and bombardments. Into it we occasionally hauled junior transgressors for a ticking-off—the moment they were outside again, and the door had closed behind them, reverting to our own badinage and gossip. During much of my career at Churcher's the common room was presided over by a stocky youth named J.G.G. Hetherington—the multiple initials somehow reinforcing the impression (which was correct) of many-sided competence, and confidence. Hetherington was our own version of the Renaissance man. He won distinctions in exams. He captained both the cricket XI and the rugby XV. He played full-back in the latter game, and when a player of the opposing side made a long kick and their scrum came roaring after the ball, we knew that Hetherington would just about always catch the ball and reverse the attack. He was a natural leader—the naturalness involving a nice sense of humor. He seemed never at a loss—no embarrassments or hesitations with Hetherington. Teachers relied on him, and so did we.

Few accounts of life in English boarding schools neglect the subject of homoerotic friendship, but—at least to my possibly blinkered vision—there seemed to be little of this at Churcher's. Occasionally we were aware that a particular boy was considered attractive, and two or three other boys were competing for his close friendship. By the time I was in my second year at Churcher's I had several good friends with whom I now and then went walking or sailing, and the only relationship I had in which there may have been an element of homosexual interest was with my housemaster, T. C. Turner. I say this with hindsight; at the time I felt at ease with him (or as much as I would have done with anyone). Now dead, he was a Yorkshireman then in his mid-forties, with gray frizzy hair, a high-pitched voice, and a loose-wristed way of gesturing; nowadays he would have immediately been identified as "gay," though in his case the condition was, I think, successfully sublimated within a real concern for his pupils. A bachelor, and the senior resident master (the headmaster had a separate house in the school grounds), he was as my housemaster required to take an interest in my progress; and when I eventually became Captain of the Grenville house, we had regular discussions about the sporting and academic events in which the four school houses competed with each other. He was also the most widely read and culturally cognizant member of the staff. He bought me several books—one, Boswell's *London Journal,* I came across again the other day and began to read again, thinking it a perceptive gift for a vain and bashful seventeen-year-old. He took me to London to see a Noel Coward musical play called *Ace of Clubs,* which I didn't think very successful, though he—a devotee of Coward—put up a strong defense for the playwright when we debated the matter on the train back to Petersfield. He even took a benevolent view of my interest in girls—though he regarded with a rather snobbish or possibly modish disdain the girls themselves, who tended to be assistants in Petersfield shops.

One girl, named Renée, used to come for walks with me on Sunday afternoons, which was the only free time boarders had during the school week. I had met her at an end-of-term dance. On our walks, the question—throbbing in my mind—of when I would take hold of her hand interfered with just about everything else, including my appreciation of the Hampshire landscape. And sometimes on my own I recognized this and told myself I was lucky that Renée had declined an invitation to come for a walk. I strode northward to Sheet and Steep, and climbed the wooded slopes, almost cliffs, called hangers, where Edward Thomas—the poet killed in France in 1917—had walked and lived and written. Or I walked south towards the gap in the Downs where the road to Portsmouth passed and where, to one side, on Butser Hill, an ancient fort displayed its mounds and embankments. I liked walking on the turfed chalk. I felt a bounce come into my step and life into my blood, and when I reached a hilltop it was tremendous to stand there breathing in the air, surveying the downs and meadows running eastward into Sussex. I returned to Churcher's along the hedged footpaths and the ploughed edges of fields, getting muddy and caught in brambles, feeling that I had stored up the natural resources with which to get through another week of school. I wondered—if walking on the Downs by oneself was such a pleasure, like sailing the Solent by oneself, why couldn't my life be arranged so that I could do just that?

# 18

"WHAT ARE YOU GOING TO BE, YANK?"

The question was directed to me one morning in the boarders' washroom, where I was standing looking at my wet face reflected in the long mirror over the row of sinks, wondering if I should conduct my once-a-week shave. I looked harder at the mirror, as the conversation about careers came to a brief halt, and though it remained unclear whether I needed to scrape a razor over my adolescent fuzz I suddenly caught my own gaze as I replied, "I am going to be a writer."

The answer—*my* answer—astonished me. The words popped out, and sounded good. But, a second later, they also sounded brash, overconfident, and of a fate-tempting kind: if that was what I really wanted to do, then I should perhaps have to sneak up on it and make fewer pronouncements. So I added, more cautiously, "Well, it's something I may have a shot at, if I can."

How I was going to become a writer, I had no idea. My published works were a couple of pieces of verse and some film reviews in *The Churcherian* and a letter in the *Portsmouth Evening News* responding to an article by the South African High Commissioner in London on the alleged advantages of apartheid. From Mr. Lane and Mr. Kershaw—marking my essays—I'd got the impression that I had some verbal facility. From books, like those of Ernest Hemingway and Negley Farson, I'd felt the glow of a craft that might blaze for one an uncommon trail, that gave a chance for an independent life—perhaps walking and sailing! Other Hampshire men had done it. Look at William Cobbett of Botley. Charles Dickens and Arthur Conan Doyle of Portsmouth and Southsea. William Thackeray of Fareham and Edward Thomas of Steep. On the other hand, I had a suspicion that to be a writer in England, even a highly regarded one, was not quite the same in terms of national admiration as being a great admiral, actor, or statesman. There was something a bit dubious, quirky and not quite proper about it. It was, moreover, a rather risky, even grubby profession: there were garrets as well as Gatsbyish mansions en route. In America, perhaps, the risk was part of the allure of literary life. From a secondhand bookshop in Petersfield I bought an out-of-date copy of *The Writers' and Artists' Yearbook,* and brooded over items about pen names and markets. "Make Writing Pay," said the advertisement of the Premier School of Journalism. In its lists of periodicals the *Yearbook* advised writers that the magazine *Aryan Path* paid eight guineas for five hundred words; *The Nation,* in New York, paid one and a half cents a word, on publication; and *The Bell,* in Dublin, published "articles by foreign writers by arrangement." I read and reread the names of publishers—The Fortune Press, Sidgwick & Jackson, Dennis Dobson—as if one might jump off the page and imprint itself on the morocco bindings of works by A. C. Bailey.

In my last term at Churcher's, the autumn term of my third year, I was one of a small group who formed the Upper Sixth. I had been made College Prefect, effectively the number three in rank under the Captain and Vice-Captain of the school. Hetherington had won entry to Cambridge. Churcher's was generally successful in getting two or three students each year into what the headmaster smugly called "one of the older universities," and perhaps several more into London University or one of the newer provincial institutions of higher education. Some boys went to the regular service colleges of Dartmouth, Sandhurst, and Cranwell, and others into professions like medicine and architecture. I was staying on for a final term to sit Oxford entrance exams. At this last moment my weight, height, and strength came into balance, and I was judged useful to the rugby team. A further qualification was a sudden access of extrovert energy. I was made leader of the scrum and, shouting loudly and melodramatically, led the Churcher's pack in muddy charges against the fifteens of Guildford, Portsmouth, Seaford, and Reading. Ours not to reason why, simply to hurl ourselves on the slippery oval ball, to push and tackle, to get bruised knees and bloody noses and stinging ears, to see our breath steaming and to stand bent and panting, hands on pink-blue thighs bandaged with mud, our striped shirts wet with sweat and drizzle. To be grateful for the final whistle. And then to come home in a coach crawling through the winter fog from a victorious away match at Bishop Wordsworth's, Salisbury, singing what we regarded as risqué songs:

> Roll me over, in the clover,
> Roll me over, lay me down, and do it again.

Then time ran out on my career as a schoolboy. Like almost all of my contemporaries, I was subject to National Service—the law required that we be conscripted for roughly two years into the armed forces. This was a duty that could be deferred until after completing a course at a university, but the accepted wisdom proposed that it might be better to get it over with and go up to university as "a more mature person," with "a broader outlook." At which point you might also have a sharper need to get something out of university life—it wouldn't be just another form of school following hard upon secondary education. At the end of the summer of 1950 I had registered and agreed to serve in the army. I was told to expect an enlistment notice shortly after I left school at Christmas. The Korean War had just begun, but I didn't immediately associate it with my own fate or that of the other 150,000 eighteen-year-olds who were called up yearly.

The state—on whose behalf I might be given the opportunity to die—had meanwhile decided to help pay for my university education. A county major scholarship was awarded to those doing well enough in the exams I had taken in June, and what I had to do now was gain entrance to a university. The Oxford exams took place in early December. They were for several different categories of entry—some with academic honors and further financial subsidies attached—and for several batches of colleges. Ration books, towels, and soap were to be brought along. I had never been to Oxford, but walking through the streets from the railway station I recognized some of the landmarks I'd seen in books and pictures: the famous towers and spires. There also seemed to be a large number of tired-looking industrial buildings and bulky gasholders. The colleges, in the wet, dark evening, were all shades of shabby gray and dirty brown. Down an alley, behind the High Street, I found Merton College, my first choice in the first four-day exams: the college entrance was through a sturdy door in a large wooden gate, with a gatehouse that reminded me of that in Portchester Castle. The fortified effect was increased by the way the crenellated buildings formed inner courtyards and quadrangles, or were linked, along the street, by a high wall topped with fierce metal spikes. Term was over, the undergraduates had gone home, and dinner in the hall was taken with thirty or forty other contestants. No one was talkative. The rooms I had been allotted were in a new, neo-Georgian set of buildings at the far end of the college, and to get there I walked through the college garden, along the high rampart that formed part of the old Oxford city walls, and past an elegant little stone summer house. It was a cold December night; the rain had stopped and mist hung over the meadows beneath the city wall. In the garden the tall trees climbed into the translucent darkness. The place was beautiful—it had never struck me before that a garden could be. In my rooms—the luxury and privacy of a bedroom and sitting room—I sat close to the electric fire, trying to reread my old school essays before the fateful test on the morrow. This was, I realized, a place where I would like to be.

Had Cicero a consistent and practical political ideal? To what extent should the intolerant be tolerated? What is propaganda, and can government be carried on without it? To what degree was Napoleon I a counterrevolutionary? Assess Parnell's achievement. *Pendant plusieurs jours de suite des lambeaux d'armée en déroute avaient traversé la ville. Eiusdem anni rem dictu parvam praeterirem, ni ad religionem visa esset pertinere.* For an English Essay: Festivals.

The ink flowed from my pen as thoughts and words provoked one another, tumbled forth. Seven terms of essay writing for Messrs. Lane, Kershaw, and Charles had brought me to this point and my replies to "not less than four questions" had to be cogently framed within the three hours given for each exam, concentrating as I had never done before, expressing anew my interest in Disraeli and Garibaldi, and dropping in at what I hoped were the right moments such adages as "Reform precedes Revolution," and statements like Canning's "I have brought a new world into existence to redress the balance of the old." "Unseen" was the name the sport of translation from Latin and French was given; I made guesses at words whose meaning I didn't know but which the context gave a few clues about, and there was always the chance of inspiration. For the essay on festivals I found myself writing an account of a visit Tony Spaeth and I had made to Dayton Fairgrounds, to a celebration commemorating Dayton's foundation as a city. In an interview the following morning with three or four dons, I said something, perhaps out of nervousness, that made them laugh; then one of them asked me about being in Ohio during the war and what effect I thought it had had upon me. I said that it had given me another family, a second country, and, in a way, a doubled past.

There was a second installment of all this for another batch of colleges, headed by Magdalen, the following week. When I got back to Churcher's, written out, it was to find a letter of congratulations from the Warden of Merton, telling me that I had been elected to a postmastership (the college's name for a scholarship) in history. Magdalen offered me entrance a week later. It was a dizzying choice to have to make between two venerable institutions: Magdalen with its tower, deer park, and riverside position, a shade more glamorous; Merton the older and more intimate, with its impressive garden and the quaintly named honor it had offered me. I plumped for Merton; the thought of it, I hoped, would be something to sustain me in the period of nearly two years before I got there. I didn't expect the glory to be long-lived.

At the end of term service in Churcher's hall, I listened to the headmaster reading out the names of boys who were leaving, with me among them, and I took a consciously final look around the walls at the portraits of former heads, photographs of cricket and rugby teams, and plaques listing the names of Old Churcherians who had died in the First and Second World Wars. Then I joined with gusto in the chorus of the school song:

> "*Credita coelo!*"
> Lustily we sing!

"*Floreant Churcheria!*"
   Make the rafters ring!

We'll pass the torch undimm'd along,
   And in all loyal endeavour,
We'll strive with zest to do our best,
   That the ship may sail for ever.

# 19

I HADN'T SEEN TONY SPAETH SINCE THAT SUMMER IN Ohio two and a half years before, but we wrote to each other occasionally and soon he was once more a handy literary device. I still had a feeling that he would understand what was going on in my mind and that he could be turned to *de profundis*. Which is where I was. "Dear Tony S.," I began my letter. "I am in the army."

Among the Christmas post that had come to Dovercot was an enlistment notice, ordering me to report to the Light Infantry Training Centre, about eight miles north of Petersfield, on a date in early January. Enclosed with the notice was a railway warrant, which I exchanged at Portchester station for a third-class single ticket. An army lorry—"truck" to you, T.S.—was waiting at Bentley station to carry me and a few fellow recruits to St. Lucia Barracks, Borden, a village given over almost entirely to the military and set in a barren, heath-covered section of north Hampshire—I might have called it featureless, but this would have been slightly at odds with the vivid fact that Borden (I soon realized) was one of the hell-holes of the universe. But I was immediately thankful to Churcher's: the experience of boarding school helped. The barracks room into which thirty of us were jammed was a colder, ruder version of the Grenville dormitory. Anyone who came to this from his own room, home comforts, and parental care was in for a sharp shock—sharper in that respect for some working-class youths who had never left their own homes. For all of us there was a sudden plunge into democratic contact; in my case,

I was in with northerners, London barrow boys, West Country building laborers, a public-school boy, and several lads who had signed on as "regulars." We looked at each other suspiciously, frostily, and eventually with mutual compassion. Each of us felt, "You poor buggers!" Some of us said it.

The spoken language was part of the novelty to me. "The fucking corporal said take the fucking broom and scrub the fucking handle with a fucking brush until the fucker's clean white, though it makes no fucking sense, if you fucking well ask me." My own innocence or prissiness was near total; then I wouldn't have even written the word (wanting to describe a loose woman I left a gap where I would have needed to use "whore," letting the context make the word understood). The closest social parallel was prison: we weren't to be allowed out of camp for the first few weeks; baggy, jail-like, denim fatigues were handed out to be worn until our uniforms were ready; we were lined up in prolonged queues for medical, dental, and mental-aptitude tests. There was an abrupt submersion in the army habit of "Hurry Up and Wait." We found ourselves hanging around for hours while the powers-that-were decided what to do with us. We found ourselves suddenly shouted at and made to double to some distant rendezvous with a quartermaster, drill sergeant, or medical officer.

I have had two really low points in my life. One, much later, was more or less self-inflicted; these first weeks of basic training were the other. The day began with noise and dread. One of our corporals woke us at 5:30 A.M. with a fearsome din of threats and imprecations. The dark disturbed by the glare of bare light bulbs. Feet on the cold floor. Mutters of "sod it" and "fucking hell" from neighboring beds. Freezing air; freezing water in the washroom; scratchy army underwear and shirts. Then form up outside and double or quick march under the pale stars—the winter dawn had not yet broken—to the mess hall, to greasy eggs, tea that tasted of metal.

The main object of the exercise was to turn us all into men who would without hesitation obey orders on the battlefield. This was accomplished in various ways, but chiefly by making us perform routine tasks to the point of perfection. Many of these tasks were connected with the care of military uniform and equipment, pressing knife-edge creases in battledress tunics and trousers, folding blankets in an intricate process called "boxing" for early-morning barracks inspection, and polishing boots and brass buckles and "Blancoing" with a light-khaki-colored clay compound our webbing, belts, and gaiters—all of this was subsumed under the title of "Bull," presumably from bullshit, and was, to a rational civilian intelligence, meaningless. One had to put out of one's mind thoughts such as "this is a complete waste of time and human energy" or "I could be doing something better with my life than this." That vacuum in the mind was something the process was intended to achieve. We were motivated, of course, by fear of punishment—in the first instance a severe dressing-down from the corporal, or in further stages by being put on a charge, finding oneself on company orders, and, in the last and worst case, "on jankers," in a punishment cell and doing hard labor. So we learned various old soldier's tricks to bring a shine to our brand-new boots—two pairs, both black and weighty, one for "best," one for everyday purposes. We used spit, polish, heat, and elbow grease; the back of a toothbrush; the back of a spoon heated with a match. I developed an antipathy that will last a lifetime for Blanco and its makers—curses on Joseph Pickering & Sons, Ltd., of Sheffield!—and for Bluebell and Brasso, the metal polishes that sometimes not only brought a shine to brass buckles and attachments but made black stains appear on the adjacent webbing—and made it necessary to repeat the Blancoing process. Unpolished brass and unclean webbing brought down the wrath of officers and NCOs at inspections. A dirty rifle was worse— "a heart-quavering experience," as I wrote to T.S. However, put on a charge, I was let off with a warning that "Next time..."

In the all-enclosing atmosphere of fear and punishment there were one or two uplifting features that allowed me (in my next letter, writing home) to say that it wasn't all bad. The stiff upper lip creasing into a faint smile would help my mother to worry less. I quickly found a few companions to grumble with and share sardonic comments on army life. ("Decent chaps," I called them, making a slight distinction from others in my platoon, who might or might not be "good lads.") Grumbling, I was later to learn, was regarded in the British army as a sign of good morale, the traditional verdict being "As long as the men are grumbling they're all right"—did Cornwallis say it at Yorktown, or Haig during the Somme? My own almost convicted status was expressed in the form Private Bailey A.C., number 22451066, but was slightly alleviated by the nightly right to wear my own striped pink, gray, and white pajamas—an item of equipment the army didn't run to—and which cheered me considerably as I climbed between the itchy army blankets. Many of the lads in my platoon didn't have pajamas! A refuge of a lackluster sort in those first few weeks was the local Navy, Army, and Air Force Institute, or NAAFI, where we could go in the evenings for tea and buns and to play table tennis. My fellow recruits yearned vocally after lustful encounters with women, generally referred to as bints (an Arabic word that the army had acquired in colonial service). The sight of one of the NAAFI girls or a few Auxiliary Territorial Service (ATS) women in the camp (who mostly looked like carthorses) led to fanciful speculations in mental striptease—my diffident suggestion that a woman could be regarded as equally beautiful with clothes on was regarded as not only high-falutin but hilarious. Some of my comrades consolingly regaled us with rich accounts of recent sessions of slap-and-tickle. (I retrieved a little prestige by showing a few barrack-room neighbors a photo Debbie Spaeth had sent me of herself, taken in the Stork Club in New York.) We took seriously the rumor that—in order to control the urges of several thousand confined young men—bromide was added to our tea.

The thought that this didn't last forever was one thing that helped get me through these dark days of basic training. Another was the possibility that I might be posted to a painless and not altogether time-wasting unit—the Education Corps was sought after in these respects. In it you became a sergeant-instructor and got sergeant's pay. You were removed from much of the tiresome routine of military life (you could wear shoes instead of boots!). The Intelligence Corps was even more highly regarded. In that you could be sent off to a university to learn, say, Russian, and wear civilian clothes most of the time. A third way out of this slough of despond was by becoming an officer—which was what I eventually decided to try to do. I applied for a "Wosbee," to appear, that is, before the War Office Selection Board, which judged potential officer material. One dilemma I detected in regard to this was that the army's basic training made for conformity—it knocked a lot of the independent rebellious youth out of you; and yet, if you wanted to be an officer, you had to show that you had some ability to think for yourself and to command your contemporaries. It was a question of identifying the right moments to assert yourself.

Meanwhile, lance-corporals yelled at us during drill, corporals raved, sergeants roared, sergeant-majors boomed, and regimental sergeant-majors made the very parade ground tremble. The army, I began to realize, was a totalitarian khaki-clad society, in which the elite or party members—the NCOs and officers—had power and everyone else had to lie low. It was an initiation in split-thinking of a kind apparently common in Eastern Europe, keeping one's mind divided into two parts, the dutiful and the free, that which obeyed and that which (quietly) thought for itself.

Parade ground; rifle range; obstacle course; route marches; inoculations; exercises in weapon handling, in stripping a Bren gun, in fire and movement, with not always very apt mnemonics to help one recall various sequences of orders—for example, GRIT: Group, who is to fire? Range, to target. Indication, of target. Type, of fire—whether slow, normal, intermittent, fast or at will. I liked some aspects of being a light infantryman—the faster pace when marching and the practice of carrying a rifle not in the sloped position over one shoulder but at the trail, suspended in the hand parallel to the ground and swinging it as one marched. (This fitted in with Eloise Spaeth's idea that one should always walk briskly, with purpose.) We had to stand up and deliver short talks (I spoke about New York and about baseball, a game in which I had taken very little interest while in the States but retained memories of, based notably on a game to which Otto had taken T.S. and me between the Cincinnati Reds and the St. Louis Cardinals, and on the film about Lou Gehrig, *Pride of the Yankees*). We went to lectures on the history of the Light Infantry regiments, to be told of heroic engagements in the Peninsular Campaign, in Afghanistan, and at Ypres. We went to hear medical officers expound, with accompanying slides, on the horrors of venereal disease (the recent reality *was* horrifying; in 1947 22.8 percent of British army personnel in Japan contracted VD, 18.5 percent in Germany). This life wasn't as I would have liked it, but I told myself there were uses in the adversity—I was having my skin thickened. No more the sensitive schoolboy.

Wearing the dark green beret and badge of the Somerset Light Infantry, I went off to the WOSB. My father, recollecting his own wartime rise from the ranks, advised me, "Make yourself heard. Show that you can give commands." Keenness must be demonstrated. We were formed into sections of eight or nine and detailed to perform various tasks—Get these packing cases across that stream as quickly as possible and without getting them wet. There was an obstacle course, and exercises in fire and movement. In the group task I remembered my performances as scrum leader, and encouraged and advised with a good deal of shouting. At lunch I sat next to a friend from Borden, Michael Newton, also a bank manager's son, who like me was aware of the fact that officers scattered around the table were keeping an ear on our conversation and an eye on our "form." It was hard not to giggle, knowing that Newton was also thinking, "They're watching to see who eats peas off his knife." Then there was an interview: a senior officer, gaunt, monocled, almost Prussian.

"Ah—Bailey. Ever in trouble in school?"

"Once or twice," I temporized, unsure what the correct answer was.

"Ever beaten for it?"

I caught on. "Yes," I lied. "Once." Leadership involved taking risks, going out on a limb now and then. I spotted what I thought was a fractional, approving nod.

Eaton Hall, near Chester, was the country home of the Duke of Westminster, who owned a great deal of Mayfair. The hall had been constantly rebuilt, its most recent manifestation being the vast Gothic palace of 1869, reminiscent of French châteaux, London railway stations, and the Palace of Westminster; it had its own clock tower, which was very like Big Ben. The current duke had owned a Derby winner and had fought with his own Rolls-Royce armored cars against the Turks in the First World War; while giving the War Office a ninety-nine-year lease on the Hall and grounds for an officer cadet school he had reserved quarters for himself in a separate wing, but we never saw him. On the main staircase, which I was to climb and descend daily, hung a huge florid painting generally referred to as "the Rubens," at which our drunken predecessors were said to hurl empty bottles on the night before their passing-out parades. There were also marble statues à la grècque in the billiards room and chinoiserie decorations in the scores of large bedrooms, in each of which four or five army beds were placed. And, at a breathtaking distance down the imposing driveway, stood an obelisk, a monument to a former duke that became a symbol of our ordeal. On the great courtyard, which was now a parade ground, the fearsome RSM Copp would detect an officer-cadet performing a movement with a smidgen less keenness than was expected. "*That man there, sergeant.*" The nearest sergeant would stride over and stamp to attention in front of the officer-cadet, whose ashen face signaled recognition of guilt and doom. The sergeant's eyes seemed to come round the sides of the peak of his cap, which, in best Guards' fashion, sloped down parallel with the bridge of his nose.

"You're an idle shower, sir," said the sergeant, his eyes enfilading the young man, and relishing as always the wonderful irony of the protocol that demanded he call an officer-cadet "sir" while permitting him to give the said officer-cadet the most almighty bollocking. "What are you, sir?"

"An idle shower, sergeant," bleated the officer-cadet.

A thunderclap came from the middle of the parade ground. "*Have him out, sergeant!*" The great barrel chest vibrated, buffeting the air. "*Round the Obelisk!*"

"Round the Obelisk, sir! At the double!" repeated the sergeant.

And the officer-cadet ran off toward the distant obelisk while the rest of us, digesting this lesson, continued even more sharply with the drill.

At Eaton Hall as at Borden, fear remained a prime mover. There was the fear of being publicly shamed in front of one's fellows. There was the fear of being relegated halfway through the four-month course back to the beginning to join the next intake—this happened to one cadet in four. And there was the overriding terror of RTU—of being returned to unit, which could happen at any time in the course of the four months, and did happen to 10 percent of us. It is curious that I had gotten through eighteen years of life—through a war, removal from my family, air raids, and submarine attacks—without being in the nervous state that the prospect of RSM Copp and the drill square induced.

Every day presented some test or other—on the square, the range, on night compass marches, and in the lecture room. We were trucked off to a camp in Wales where we spent a fortnight under canvas in bad weather. There were nighttime maneuvers. We had a week's so-called battle camp on Dartmoor to look forward to as a final test; there, it was said, we would come under fire from live ammunition. I wrote home: "There is a tense atmosphere here at the Hall, and while it would be exaggerating to say that everyone is acting, many are, and it is hard to play the leader and officer all the time." I did well in most of the written exams and less well in "action," where public coherence and an incisive, rapidly gathered view of a tactical situation were necessary.

There were a few compensations. At Borden, once

we were no longer confined to barracks, I had used some of my free time to walk to villages which, though not many miles away, made the army seem remote. I walked to Selborne, where the naturalist Gilbert White had lived, and to Chawton, Jane Austen's village. I trudged along footpaths, had lunch in pubs, and sat in old churches, happy to be alone. At Eaton Hall we had the occasional evening and most weekends free. I caught a bus to Chester and walked around the city. I walked along the city wall and thought of the wall that formed on its inner side an embankment along the edge of Merton's garden. I walked in the Rows, the upstairs and downstairs arrangement of arcaded, double-deck passages for shoppers and pedestrians. I went to mass in the morning in a Catholic church and, later in the day, to Chester Cathedral, a strong-looking pink sandstone edifice, for evensong—was the army turning me back to the consolations of religion? I went to a supper club and danced with a retroussé-nosed Welsh girl called Mair, a name which suddenly seemed to me much prettier than Poppy or Renée. And, since summer had arrived, I went to Heswall on the river Dee to go sailing. Commander Hamond knew a yacht designer named Peter Brett who lived at Heswall with his family—and the Bretts in the friendly way of sailors looking after one of their own arranged for me to have the use of a racing dinghy at the Dee Sailing Club. There, on half a dozen weekends, I had all the pleasures and anxieties of boat proprietorship while racing and voyaging down the tidal estuary of the Dee, and facing small disasters like the rudder falling off at the start of a race. I went for picnics on sandbanks with the Bretts and dinner with the club commodore, his wife, and his daughter. As usual I found that the apprehensions of sailing blotted out all other worries—RSM Copp, relegation, RTU—with my imagination absorbed in the way the tiller felt in my hand, the sounds the boat made moving through the water, and the effect on the boat's speed of changing the angle of heel or set of its sails.

Several times I was accompanied to Heswall by a fellow cadet, Andrew Sedgemore. Andrew was in my company at Eaton Hall and was planning to go on to New College, Oxford, to read history. He had a positive, determined manner and a good deal of intellectual curiosity; his "leadership potential," to look at it in army terms, was obvious—he had been made an under-officer, which was like being a prefect at school in relation to ordinary officer-cadets. In a boat, our positions were reversed—I was the skipper. Hitchhiking to Heswall or on other occasions into Wales, to swim on the beaches or climb through Mount Francon Pass into the mountains, we were disputatious equals. We threw at each other the names of books, historians, and poets. Andrew had the useful trait of not accepting at face value remarks made to him, however passionate or considered, and I found myself having to furnish examples and argument to back up my opinions. Andrew had been to one of the best public schools; his father was managing director of a large company; but his grandfather had begun his working life as a humble railwayman.

"Now, this man Yeats," said Andrew. "You're always going on about him. A great poet, perhaps. But an awful lot of spiritualist nonsense attached—like table-tapping and phoney séances."

"Oh, come on—I wouldn't say attached. It's woven in, it was necessary to him, and it is colorful, beautiful."

"Beautiful!" snorted Andrew. "Tell me what that means." (He had his own need to call things beautiful but a greater need just then to be the devil's advocate.) We might be talking like this while going to a Saturday-night dance in Heswall, where—leaving Yeats aside for the moment—we would both make determined attempts to convince the local girls that we were impressive fellows, though they were more interested in the more permanent local lads.

It was a time when letters to and from home mattered. The post was cheap and fast—I sent shirts to be laundered by my mother and got them back almost by return mail. I tried to convince my parents that a motorcycle would make it possible for me to get home for the weekend on a forty-eight-hour pass, and that my future pay as an officer would cover the cost of a secondhand 350 c.c. machine on which I would swoop down to Portchester—if my father would lend me the purchase price. This, obviously, was when I was feeling optimistic about my chances of passing out as an officer at the end of the course. Writing home was also a refuge, something I did at the end of a nerve-racking day of being commanded by NCOs and being asked for sudden decisions by officers. I would sit, almost in hiding, in a corner of the Hall's fine library, with a letter pad or my volume of Yeats. Poetry provided a personal dugout, in all sorts of circumstances. I sat by myself on the beach at Rhyl, where I had gone in the hope of running into Mair, and scribbled some verses; but I didn't keep them.

Like many periods of difficulty, that time came to seem valuable for having provided a parcel of knowledge that one would never otherwise have come by, and which gave one experiences and a craft shared with others who went through it. Now, if I am in Yorkshire for the weekend and walking with a friend who is a university teacher of politics (and who earlier went to Sandhurst and held a regular army commission for five years), I know that as we enter a dip between two low hills he will in all likelihood suddenly say, "Platoon in attack! The situation: The dead ground is in that direction. I will place my covering section on hillock A, over there. Sections one and three will move forward at 1335 hours and capture the copse at map reference XYZ." So I still on occasion see a landscape not only in terms of farming utility, of wild or cultivated beauty, but in terms of where I would place my mortar group to provide smoke to cover the advance, or where the Bren guns should be sited to keep the enemy's heads down as we attack.

I enter into the spirit of these military exercises even if the memories they provoke aren't all associated with success. Toward the end of the sixteen-week course we were sent from Eaton Hall to the week-long battle camp on Dartmoor. It was understood that this was to be the ultimate test, the toughest part of the course, and that there would be a final weeding-out. We took turns at running the platoon, and in commanding it during fire-and-movement exercises, to demonstrate that we had mastered the techniques of handling thirty infantrymen during a battle. Platoon in attack, as it was called. My turn came. The platoon was advancing under my command across the rugged moorland, the southwest wind blowing fresh and clouds hurtling across the sun; but I wasn't giving much thought to the pleasures of the landscape, of the gorse and grass. I knew that any moment our instructor, Captain Rutherford, would set off a thunderflash—a very noisy firework—to signal that we were under fire. When he did so, I was still surprised. I went to ground, as did the rest of my platoon. I crawled forward to join Rutherford and peer from behind a prickly gorse bush at the terrain ahead. "You are under fire from a position on the upper slope of that tor over there," said Rutherford, crisply—he was a trim figure who wasted little time on smiles and courtesies. "The enemy are about twenty strong and have a machine gun and a mortar which is firing at you, *now!*"

The "*now!*" was designed to impel immediate action, and it got me in haste to a crouching position behind a nearby gorse bush that offered a similar vantage point.

I yelled to some members of my platoon to disperse; they were bunched together, furnishing too neat a target. Then I signaled to the cadet who had been designated my runner, and he dashed over to join me. Together we formed the observation group for the platoon. I was now meant to "appreciate" the situation, to make a plan of attack, and then deliver it to my "orders group"—the platoon sergeant, three section commanders, and the NCO in charge of the mortar squad.

Here things began to go fuzzy. It was like one of those debates in school, where the words were all in my head, but there were too many of them and they didn't seem to be coming forth in the right order. I was conscious of the gorse pressing into one knee. I was aware of Rutherford nearby, staring at the ground, listening to what I was saying. My orders group had gathered around and were looking at me expectantly—how is he going to handle it? Is he going to make a botch of it?

I remembered most of the sequence of orders. I gave out information about the enemy, about my intention of taking and destroying the enemy position, and about my method of attack. I sounded as though I was trying to remember things, which detracted from the firmness with which—we had been told—orders should be delivered. I dispatched one section to provide covering fire. I led the other two sections to make the attack. And here things began to go really wrong. Partly it was a matter of timing, of coordinating the assault with the moment at which my fire section was to open up with its blank rounds. Partly it was the direction from which, a bit disoriented by the ground, I led my attacking sections in upon the enemy position. Rutherford met me on the edge of their hypothetical entrenchments. "Right, Bailey, you can halt your men and stand them easy. They are all dead. You have just made your attack right into your own covering fire."

There were several more platoon-in-attack exercises that day, commanded by others. Returned to being a cog in the machine, I had no chance to shine or make amends. I could see the letters RTU being typed after my name on company orders. To have come this far...

Rutherford formed us up in the middle of the afternoon. We were exhausted. He didn't seem pleased by the way the day had gone. I found myself with a Bren gun to carry—equipment I'd inherited from the closing exercise—and I wasn't looking forward to lugging it the three miles or so back to camp in Okehampton.

"Okay," said Rutherford. "You marched out here. Just to make things different, it's going to be a cross-country run on the way back. I shall be interested in seeing who is first man home."

I had never been fond of running; that was my father's talent. In cross-country runs at Churcher's I had struggled around the course, the leaders well out of sight, and could remember the panting, the buzzing in the brain, the hallucinations, the leaden limbs. Here, I knew, it was one of those occasions when one's life is made or unmade. The die was almost cast. We moved off at a fast jog. I heard my boots pound, my heart pound. I moved the Bren occasionally, carrying it sometimes at the trail, sometimes at the "present" position, across the chest. Soon we were in a long drawn-out line—I was somewhere in the middle of it—following a footpath, having to clear stiles and dodge cowpats, then coming down a lane, the boots sounding louder now, the pounding going all through me, and Rutherford, weaponless, trotting easily, the sort of man who played squash and ran daily, and the line getting longer, the gaps between the battledress-clad runners getting wider. But I was keeping up. I was in the first stretched-out bunch of ten or so. One, red in the face, nodded to me, made a mute offer to take the Bren in exchange for his rifle. I made the barest shake of the head, wasting no energy in saying no. I could see the spire of Okehampton church. The hedges familiar. The camp in view. Sweat. Air. I was in fact passing people. A dip, an ascent, a dip. The camp gates. The huts.

Rutherford trotted in, flushed but by no means extended. He gave us a chance to stand bent, hands on knees, chests heaving. The Bren gun stood, bipod open, beside me. Rutherford had come in behind the first half dozen; then the others had straggled in.

"Who was here first?"

I hadn't the wind to speak consecutive words. I heard a cadet named Jenkins say, between pants. "Bailey and I, sir—a dead heat"—which was charitable of him; I was sure he had just beaten me. Rutherford said curtly, "Well done." He gave me a laconic look in which I read, through sweat-clouded eyes, a change of heart.

# 20

AT THE PASSING OUT SERVICE IN EATON HALL CHAPEL the first hymn was John Bunyan's. The first reading given by the chaplain was nicely chosen: "They that wait upon the Lord shall renew their strength, they shall mount up with wings as eagles: they shall run and not be weary: they shall walk and not faint." Poor bloody infantry! I was commissioned as a second lieutenant in the Wiltshire Regiment, Wiltshire being a county in which I had never set foot. We had been asked to give our suggestions as to where we would like to be posted. The British army was well scattered still around the globe. A large number were serving in Germany as the Army of the Rhine, but Germany seemed accessible enough to see at any time. Korea, where the war was a year old and where British regiments like the Gloucesters were fighting gallantly, was not going to figure among my choices. Somewhere like Bermuda or the Bahamas would be a great fluke, a really cushy posting—my friend Sedgemore landed such an assignment, being sent to Hong Kong. I thought about Egypt, which might be an interesting part of the world to see at government expense, and was relieved a few months later that I hadn't gone there, when riots and general commotion broke out in the Canal Zone and we Brits were actually being shot at. East Africa, particularly Kenya, took my fancy, though my research into the King's African Rifles—the regiment I applied to be posted to—failed to uncover the fact that some of the KAR were serving in Malaya, where terrorists and insurgents infested the jungles and something like a civil war was going on. In Kenya, moreover, the KAR's home base, a native organization called the Mau Mau had recently been proscribed and all sorts of mayhem was about to break out.

In fact, the War Office pondered me and my record and decided: not East but West Africa; not the King's African Rifles but the Royal West African Frontier Force, and specifically that part of it known as the Third Battalion of the Gold Coast Regiment. I was given a week's leave—time to go home to Portchester and have a few sails in a borrowed Duck (I'd sold *Rhapsody* at the end of the previous season). In Plymouth, where I reported to the Wessex Group Training Centre for documentation, the Lieutenant Colonel talked to me about T. S. Eliot—had I read *Four Quartets?* Wasn't it interesting that the Dry Salvages were really *les Trois Sauvages,* a group of rocks off Cape Ann, Massachusetts? Then London, where I reported to the military Movement Office deep in Goodge Street underground station, where for some reason it had stayed since the war, as if still hiding from enemy air attack. I bought some tropical-weight shirts and shorts at Moss Bros. and went to see Cole Porter's *Kiss Me Kate;* TCT, my ex-housemaster, would have liked it (I thought it slightly arch).

I flew to Africa from Blackbushe, one of the smaller suburban airfields that had been useful during the war—one still thought of them as aerodromes. The plane was a Viking, Britain's answer to the Dakota. Single seats on one side of the aisle, double seats on the other, filled mostly with army wives and children. Bordeaux was the first stop, for fuel, and Gibraltar the second, where we stayed the night. Then off next morning across the gleaming straits, above the mountains of Morocco, and over the vast desert, with funnels of heat shooting up, the plane rising and sinking like an elevator, the small children crying and airsick bags in demand. We came down to refuel at a French staging post somewhere in the Sahara, the heat so thick you could barely see through it—and what I saw, walking slowly on the edge of the sandy airstrip, looked like a mirage: a wavering image of a fort, a tricolor, a legionnaire in baggy trousers and burnous. The next stop was Gao, on the Niger, a little way east of Timbuktu—the place which as a child I had thought of as more remote than anywhere. In Gao the heat was wetter and everybody was black. Last, Accra.

The Third Battalion of the Gold Coast Regiment—3 GCR—provided the force that protected various establishments in and around the Gold Coast capital. It guarded Government House, which had once been Christiansborg Castle, a fortified Danish trading post, where the governor, Sir Charles Arden-Clarke, now lived. It guarded military stores depots and various buildings at the cantonments where the battalion was based. It provided ceremonial guards for the opening of Parliament. And, like any infantry unit, it trained, went on maneuvers, and conducted rifle practice on the ranges. My job as a platoon commander was to lead and supervise my men—an African sergeant and thirty African other ranks—in these duties, to command them on parade, to visit them when they were serving as guards, and to deal with any worries they had about pay, food, or living conditions; to be, in fact, at the age of nineteen, suddenly *in loco parentis* to men who were older and used to the ways of a different world, from which I was cut off.

Most of them were from Ashanti, in the mid-section of the country, or from the Northern Territories; they had joined the army for food, clothing, and a conical thatched hut to live in. They spoke among themselves their own languages, Ga or Ashanti, and to us Europeans a pidgin English—in which we often found ourselves replying. They wore when in uniform red fezes on their heads—I wore a light-khaki-colored felt slouch hat, Australian style, with a wide brim turned up on one side and a green plume rising from it. I wore long socks with my shorts; the men wore puttees that were rolled up around their legs from ankle to knee, and that made their legs look like the trunks of palm trees. I lived in a giddah, a one-room bungalow in the junior officers' lines. The officers' mess and parade ground were nearly a mile up the road, forming part of the Cantonments, where the men lived in their own lines in their small, round, whitewashed huts; most of the men were married and had their wives and children with them. A few Africans, Sandhurst-trained, were among the officers, but most of these were British regulars and war veterans. The terms black and white were not much used—"African" and "European" were; and distinctions were drawn between British and African enlisted men in terms and conditions of service. I rose early, wakened by my personal servant—who would have been called a batman in Britain but was called a boy here—bringing me a cup of tea and hot water for shaving. We were employed on military duties during the very long morning and then had the afternoon off; it was too hot for much of anything. We were expected to dine in the officers' mess most nights. If one had the twenty-four-hour task of being duty or orderly officer, one was required to drive round Accra in a Land-Rover at some time during the night, turning out the guards at various locations to ensure that they were on their toes.

It strikes me now that perhaps the waves of bad temper that I often felt surging down on me from my superior officers were caused by their unexpressed belief that the whole performance—the very fact of them being in the Gold Coast—was a waste of time. For a professional long-service officer it was not a desirable posting. No doubt they were also affected by realizations of the recent drift of history: the Empire and this sort of late colonial soldiering were on the way out. There had been a state of emergency in the Gold Coast a year and a half before I got there, with strikes and other forms of civil disorder. The first election for a parliamentary assembly had recently been held, giving the Convention People's Party of Kwame Nkrumah a huge majority. As in other places where the sun was slowly setting on imperial power, the leader of the nationalist movement had been spending time in prison, but on being elected prime minister Dr. Nkrumah was let out of jail. One of my duties as a junior officer of 3 GCR was training my troops in riot drill—Duties in Aid of the Civil Power, as it was euphemistically called. I had to decide at what point I should read out through a megaphone the warning on the yellow card, calling on the rioters to disperse in the king's name. When to shoot over their heads. How to pinpoint the ringleaders. I didn't look forward to having to put any of this into practice.

In fact, I felt as fragmented by the Gold Coast and my subaltern's role as I'd ever felt; the army didn't have the whole me. I sometimes wished that I could carry out my duties with polish and precise good manners, in the way that a few of my contemporaries did, instead of feeling boorish and sulky. ("Crosspatch!" was what Bridget had called me on occasion; the army made me feel cross quite often.) But perhaps memory exaggerates the number of times when these feelings showed. Much of the time I put an effort into being agreeable and competent. The trouble was that the place itself demanded notice in a way that the army, in its inert, possessive manner, was ill equipped for allowing me to take. "You don't want to get interested in all that"—meaning all the local, native, African things that interested me—was the military message; just do your job diligently and everything will be uncomplicated.

My morning uniform was the slouch hat and starched khaki shirt and shorts; the evening kit on mess nights when we had formal dinners, once or twice a week, was black tie, black dinner-dress trousers, scarlet cummerbund, suede mosquito boots, and starched white monkey-jacket with the regimental insignia fastened to the lapels. Stiffness was evident also in conversation and the constriction of mess etiquette—and, in reaction, in the coarse jokes and boyish roughhousing that sometimes followed the Royal toast. However, on Sundays after church parade we could drive to Labadi beach to swim in the high surf. The huge rollers shot me ashore or, if I judged them wrongly, pounded me against the shelving bottom. Then, at the lunch table the mess had brought to the beach, we ate vast quantities of curry and drank the local beer, which was called Club and came in tall green bottles. I took up smoking. Cigarettes could be bought cheaply in round tins of fifty, and I experimented happily with Capstan, Craven A, Du Maurier, Players, Rothmans, Churchmans, Senior Service, Turkish Ovals, Passing Cloud, Abdullahs, Balkan Sobranie, and Black Russian Sobranie, which had gold tips. The intention was to achieve poise and the nonchalance, languid or laconic, of the heroes of Noel Coward or Raymond Chandler. I tried various drinks. I learnt that six champagne cocktails (made of champagne and brandy) drunk at a mess celebration gave one, next morning, the world's worst hangover.

Craving excitement, contact with young women, and distance from the mess, I went out some evenings with my fellow subalterns. We went looking for Accra night life. This was to be found in contrasting forms. That which suited our early sobriety was the lounge of the Avenida Hotel, where the music reminded me of the Young Conservative socials and where, dared by my friends Peter Carhill and Peter Hooker, I asked a girl to dance (she was tall and supple, like Iris Rutledge; she was the first black girl I'd ever talked to; she told me she was a secretary as we did a foxtrot. But conversation didn't exactly flow, and she declined an invitation to join us at our table). As the evening wore on, we moved to seedier haunts. "Take us somewhere really low and shocking," we said to Mensah, our driver, and so we ended up at places like "Weekend in Havana" and "Springtime in the Rockies"—hole-in-the-wall bars whose expansive ambitions were manifested in flickering neon signs, concrete dance floors lit by a string of naked light bulbs, and combos that played High Life, the local fusion of jazz and Gold Coast rhythm, to which dancers did a sort of jitterbug. We didn't attempt the High Life, but sat at the bar, drinking rather suspicious Dutch-labeled whisky while listening to one of the few other white customers, grizzled veterans of the Coast who could be found in such places, foremen for big construction projects or agents for cocoa buyers, and who as the night progressed became confessional, needing to tell tales of success and failure, boondoggles and bonanzas—all of which was gripping at the time but hard to remember the next morning.

The army was paying me for my modest services, and a monthly sum was credited to my bank account. After I had paid my mess bills there was something left over; it was exciting to have one's own small income and be able to spend it. I found a Syrian tailor's shop near the central market, where the traders sold bright lengths of cotton called mammy cloth—in which the Gold Coast women swaddled themselves—and where women so clad hawked vegetables and sat at small charcoal stoves, frying plantains for eating on the spot. The tailor was in a row of concrete buildings, given over to small workshops on the ground floor, with roll-down shutters instead of doors and windows, selling car parts and making furniture. I ordered a smoking jacket to my own design, with rolled lapels and patch pockets, made of plum-red corduroy (cheaper than velvet) and presumably intended to enhance my bohemian chances in after-dark Accra; it would undoubtedly shock Portchester when I returned. Eloise had sent me some books (Sinclair Lewis, Sherwood Anderson) and I had joined a book club, which started by sending me *Emma* and *Moll Flanders.* So I bought a small iroko bookcase to house these cherished volumes, and stood on top of it another new possession, an ivory-colored radio that, with the help of a wire as an aerial led into the rafters of my giddah, brought in Radio Brazzaville, Lagos, and the BBC Overseas Service. Watched by a praying mantis, which also inhabited the rafters and which looked like several green pencils joined weirdly together, I sat during my domestic evenings and let the world expand.

I bought a motorcycle. It was the first of three, a yellow and green BSA Bantam. It was small and low-powered, but good for beginning—or would have been if the 125 c.c. engine hadn't had a terminal condition in its bearings. I confronted on his bank premises the young European bank clerk who had sold it to me, and—since the bank was not the place where he wanted a scene—achieved a small repayment. For a few weeks after that I was the owner of a big Ariel 500, an ex-army machine that was powerful and noisy—and hard to start. I sold it to a sergeant (British) who had greater experience with motorcycles and in its place bought a BSA 350—fast enough and handsome with its shiny black paint and chrome; it quickly proved its worth as a means of escape from the battalion. I no longer spent the afternoons in my giddah but roared up the road to Achimota University College, eight miles north of the cantonments, or wandered off on narrow tracks into the countryside, "the bush." The young Engineers officer who sold it to me, just before being sent back to England, told me after several drinks that the BSA had taken him to a village where he had become chummy with the chief, and the chief—after the young man had participated in several ceremonies—had given him one of his daughters. No directions for finding the village had been offered, and I didn't ask for them; perhaps the BSA, given its head, would find its way there. When I told Peter Hooker about this (Hooker had been on the Coast a few months longer than me), he said that the previous owner of the motorbike had clearly gone bush—that is to say, had become obsessed with the place and native ways. It was a condition, akin to madness or malaria, that struck Europeans from time to time, particularly those who stayed on the Coast more than a year. But although we were given quinine pills to take daily against malaria, against going bush there was no known prevention. A case cropped up soon after this. We heard of an officer from Command headquarters who had bought a bottle of Gordon's gin from his mess and had joined the chief of a fishing village near Labadi in making a libation to the sea god, throwing the unopened bottle into the surf.

Achimota had a good bookshop and a hospitable library. I introduced myself diffidently, not yet an undergraduate, an officer of the occupying power in afternoon civvies, but was shown how to work the cataloguing system and given a place to sit while I read about the history and traditions of the region, former empires, invasions, migrations. In 1594 the Songhai Empire had been invaded from Morocco; cultural objects had been plundered, including literary artifacts, and the ruling class massacred and dispersed. As a result, the Songhai people migrated southward. They ran into another movement then affecting the coast—the Portuguese, Dutch, and English who in turn were exploring, setting up trading and slaving posts, and building fortifications.

It was by no means as complicated as English history, but a good deal more so than I'd expected. And when I'd grasped the general pattern I began to delve into specialist works, while the library's overhead fans stirred the humid air. In one book on West African religion, I read about Captain R. S. Rattray, an English anthropologist who early this century did research among the Ashanti tribes living in the middle of what by then had become the Gold Coast Colony. Rattray, it seemed, was the only white man to have reached a temple near the source of the river Tano. One of the great rivers of the country, the Tano was venerated as a god in both the Gold Coast and adjoining Ivory Coast. Sometimes Tano was credited with creation. Sometimes he was said to be the second son of the supreme God, 'Nyame. The temple Rattray had found was at a village called Tano Oboase, which meant Tano beneath the rock.

As I rode the BSA back toward the Cantonments that evening—a mess night; I would have to get kitted out for dinner—I decided that I would go looking for Rattray's temple.

# 21

IN EARLY FEBRUARY THE KING DIED—FRAIL, SHY GEORGE VI, whom it was hard to recall except in terms of photographs of wartime visits to blitzed streets, his plump, sweetly smiling wife beside him, for all his obvious unease and difficulties with public speaking an endearing figure. It was easy to sympathize with him for not wearing the crown as if it suited him—clearly it had dropped on him out of the blue. Nevertheless he had been our head of state, and had personified Britain's problems throughout the 1940s—smoking too much, stuttering, looking thinner and thinner. For a moment, as I listened on my radio to the announcements of mourning and expressions of sympathy, I thought about England.

The Gold Coast had only two seasons. One, lasting from May to September, was hot and wet; the other was hot and dry. The hot, rainy season began with a sort of spring: new growth, and occasional periods of coolness that came with the rain. Although Accra, we were told, wasn't as wet as places further inland, its rain was impressive. This was nothing like an English drizzle or even what in England was called a downpour. Here rain felt like the bottom falling out of a swimming pool; the roadside gutters, meant to cope with such deluges, were deep concrete trenches, partially roofed at street level to prevent pedestrians and vehicles falling in. With the wet season the local insect life, never subdued, sallied forth in strength. One could hear the voices of a million crickets from the grassland along the road to the mess. I made a dash, after undressing, to get into bed, where I pulled the mosquito net tight, listening for the hum that indicated that one of the raiders had penetrated the defensive screen.

The new season also brought battalion reorganizations. The commanding officer, a lieutenant colonel, was to be posted back to Britain to assume command of a detention barracks, a position to which I considered he was eminently suited. The adjutant, who remained, took delivery of a Jaguar drophead roadster and roared in and out of the cantonments, looking (we subalterns thought) more of a stuck-up s.o.b. than ever. It was perhaps he who decided that I should be sent for three months, with my platoon, to demonstrate basic infantry tactics at the West African Command Training School near the fishing village of Teshie. Whether this secondment was an honor or the adjutant and C.O. wanted to get rid of me, I couldn't decide. A perceptive reading of my record, and particularly any contribution Rutherford may have made to it, might have led the adjutant to say, as he got to the end of my performance on Dartmoor, "Bailey's the chap for this." On the other hand, a verdict arrived at in that way—with the impulse for irony displacing a desire for military efficiency as the determining factor—could be injurious to the training of future platoon commanders of the West African Frontier Force. Yet again, maybe that was what he had in mind. Though I didn't give him credit for much imagination and foresight, he might have thought ahead to the time when this battalion became a unit in the army of an independent African state, and decided that irony, if not actual sabotage, was in order.

Teshie was a collection of huts and houses several miles east of Accra, on the coast road, within sound of the surf. The training school had other, immediately perceptible advantages. I was—except for occasional attendance at formal battalion functions—liberated from

3 GCR activities. I had my own little command, albeit within the training-school structure. I was out from under the avuncular wing of my company commander, George Lane. The afternoons were even freer at Teshie. I continued to visit Achimota and also started a correspondence course in Spanish— "Beginners are inclined to use the nominative pronouns too much," warned the notes to lesson six. I translated passages on subjects like the four seasons, but began to run out of enthusiasm at lesson seven; perhaps *I* didn't see the language's relevance to *myself*. There was now an I whom I wanted to express: stumbling things got written during those Teshie afternoons, some in verse, some in prose, some in inchoate minglings of both forms. I wrote about the rain and the heat, the two dominant elements here that pushed man into a humble and undetermining place, except possibly as an observer. The boast or hope uttered in the Churcher's washroom still resounded in memory; I bought a small metal-cased portable typewriter and assured myself that I would earn its cost with what got written on it.

The local literary market didn't require a profound survey. It consisted of the Accra *Daily Graphic,* a thin tabloid owned by a British newspaper group but staffed by Africans. Short items of what to me were obscure pieces of reportage appeared among advertisements for Sloan's Liniment and Dr. Morse's Indian Root Pills. One or two of the local cinemas showed Arabic films but the staple fare was westerns: *Billy the Kid's Range War* and *Saddle Tramp,* starring Joel McCrea and Wanda Hendrix, were two that were showing on the day the *Graphic* published my first article, which made a shallow attempt to analyze the lure of cowboy films and present a capsule history of the opening-up of the American West: phrases like "virgin forest," "tradition-bound Eastern states," "the rich plains," "the slow unfolding of the nineteenth century..." "Meet the tough men of the West," said the headline, giving me early warning of the truth that subeditors generally have something else in mind when it comes to telegraphing the substance of what appears below. It didn't matter, of course; the cliché I was trying to rebut wasn't much greater than the platitudes I used in the rebuttal, however disguised in what I imagined were pithy, hard-hitting sentences. I was nevertheless proud of my first published work, which was credited to Anthony Cooper—a pen name chosen less out of modesty than from anxiety about mixing writing for the local press with my military career. (But I had to tell a few people, like Nigel McKeand and John Heritage, fellow junior officers at Teshie, who thereupon mystified the adjutant by toasting me one night as Six-gun Bailey. My expertise with weapons had hitherto been well concealed.) I went down to the *Graphic* offices to talk to the assistant editor, Bankole Timothy, about getting paid for my piece and about future assignments. I had ideas about becoming the *Graphic*'s European reporter while I was at university, sending back for Gold Coast readers searing pieces about real life among the towers and spires. Mr. Timothy told me that he had arranged for a cheque for one guinea to be sent to me and that he would very much like to see more of my work. Before coming to Africa the only black man I had known had been James, the Spaeths' butler-chauffeur, and whatever my liberal convictions concerning black-white relations, as expressed in my letter about apartheid to the Portsmouth *Evening News*, the fact was I had been exposed almost entirely to situations where the white man had a dominant role. Now, in this shabby, cluttered office (I think Bankole Timothy wrote half the paper on most days), I found myself being encouraged to write by a friendly man in his mid-thirties who just happened to be black.

The afternoons at Teshie also gave me time to jot down in an army exercise book quotations from writers who impressed me. I was susceptible to oratory, moved by sweeping statements if expressed with sufficient panache. Medieval mystics and murky Russian philosophers made me wonder. I was still going to mass occasionally but had decided that no church could claim that it had the one way to God, or even the right to insist on one God. Here in West Africa people not only worshiped rivers like the Tano but felt the gods existed in phenomena like the seasons and diseases, or natural objects like iroko trees and snakes. Daily offerings were put in pots hung in the branches of trees; before drinking palm wine, it was the custom to pour a little on the ground so that one's ancestors could drink first. As I stood on the veranda of my Teshie giddah, listening to the surf from the beach or, at night, looking up at the clear and brilliant mass of stars, I found it hard to go on thinking in terms of the Christian God—whether Father Frawley's or John Bunyan's—who allegedly took an interest in us His Children. Surely the only way one could explain the mysteries of the universe, and answer such questions as Who made us and Why, was by assuming that *we,* too, were God. We were small particles of the Deity—the Creator; minute atoms of creation in constant change, perhaps proceeding by way of birth, growth, decay, and destruction toward an infinite refinement and perfection.

My disquiet on this subject was reflected in physical restiveness. I applied for local leave. I had to visit the battalion to do this, and Smallwood, the adjutant of 3 GCR, let me know at once that he thought it a mistake that the War Office allowed leave to National Service officers—after all, I had only another four months to serve. However, as I was entitled to two weeks, he assumed that I would take it at a time convenient to the battalion and at a suitable place, such as the Officers' Rest Camp at Sekondi Beach west of Accra. What I hoped to do, however, was first to reconnoiter the old forts and castles along the coast, and then go looking for the Tano temple. I was relieved that Smallwood had failed to note I would miss the Monarch's Birthday Parade, an annual military event made more important this June by being in honor—for the first time in fifty years—of a Queen. Meanwhile my motorcycle rides took me increasing distances out of town. I followed the red laterite roads until they became tracks and then narrow paths, winding through the bush, sometimes hollowed out by wear and rain into gullies and trenches. Motorcycle helmets were neither common nor legally necessary. I generally rode bare-headed. But I was glad I was wearing army boots on the occasion of the one accident I had, when the motorbike ran suddenly into a narrow gully and one of my feet, sticking out from the footrest, was twisted sharply round, almost back to front—a bad sprain; nothing broken.

Through constant repetition of exercises, my platoon and I began to achieve a certain competence. We demonstrated platoon tactics to groups of African NCOs and a few African second lieutenants, sent to Teshie from various Gold Coast and Nigerian units. We demonstrated firing on the ranges, the teaching of mortar and machine-gun operation, the art of map reading and organization of a compass march. My platoon sergeant, Sergeant Seidu, was from the Northern Territories, whose harsher climate seemed to be expressed in his shaved scalp and benign, almost purified manner—which I compared with the Westernized and sometimes more devious ways of the Coast people and the earthier, slower manner of the Ashanti. Sergeant Seidu helped me elicit from the men what there was to be got. And in the same way that an experienced European NCO would have done, he managed to convey to his young officer—this lanky white youth—when he thought the pressure of command might be counterproductive or when certain maneuvers might need to be simplified in order to succeed—though, like many Africans, he made these suggestions as much through silence as through dissent. As I repeated my commands, I rephrased and abbreviated. Sometimes Sergeant Seidu translated my orders into a native tongue from the simple English I was using, though occasionally I wove into it phrases of pidgin English picked up from the men. Much of the time I got on with my platoon the way I would have done with English soldiers, but there were more definite limits to my knowledge of them and powers of identification with them. Ordinary problems of pay, clothing, food, and dependents weren't insurmountable, and here, as in Britain, what was put forward as a material problem sometimes disguised another, more private concern. Probably among British enlisted men I would have sensed, or made a stab at finding out, what underlay the difficulty. Here, as I asked a question that was meant to get to the bottom of it all, the large, moist, dark eyes would shift and the personality being probed would retreat into unreachable depths. Once, on a long route-march in the country where the coastal grasslands began to give way to low hills and forest, I thought I had got us lost, but as we descended a hillside into an orange grove, realized we were where we were meant to be. We picked oranges from the trees. My light khaki shirt was as sweat-darkened as their equally damp darker khaki shirts. We shared with smiles the relief that we had got somewhere together.

The demonstration platoon was picked for a starring role in a Military Tattoo to be held on Accra Racecourse. The army was going to show off its skills to the people—and particularly to the governor-general and the recently elected prime minister, Dr. Kwame Nkrumah. On several afternoons we went to rehearse on the grassed area inside the track. In front of the grandstand, out in the middle of the grass, a small concrete hut formed our objective; it represented an enemy pillbox. When the attack section had taken the pillbox, it would blow it up—an action to be simulated on the night of the Tattoo by setting off a thunderflash. Then I and my men would continue our advance across the racecourse.

The rehearsals went well. It was a straightforward platoon attack, running and then crawling, with a fire section out on a flank providing covering fire with blank ammo. The ground, being flat, provided no opportunity for mistakes of the kind I'd made on Dartmoor. On the night itself, under the floodlights of the racecourse, after the bands had played and 3 GCR had marched past, all went well with our little demonstration until my attack party and I reached the pillbox. We went inside and I got out the thunderflash and matches. Then, having presumably accounted for the defenders, we stepped out of the door at the rear. I prepared to light the giant firework and throw it into the pillbox. Army-issue matches, meant to be waterproof. I struck one—no flame. Another—same result. A third—nothing. The matches were damp, dud, useless. War stock, perhaps; been to India and back. "Anyone got any matches?" I whispered as loudly as I could. No. I shouted, "Come on!" to my team, and waved on the rest of the men who had been waiting for the *bang* as a signal to advance. Those who saw and heard advanced; the others gradually got the picture and straggled after us into the gloom at the edge of the course.

"Bit anticlimactic, Bailey," said Major Watson, the Training Centre C.O. He was a walrus-mustached, choleric-cheeked officer whom I tried to encounter as rarely as possible. "What was the reason for that fiasco?"

Clearly the colonel had been onto him; the general had been onto the colonel; the governor-general had been onto the general. How could the prime minister and his gang be expected to think *anything* of us if we couldn't even perform the ceremonial blowing-up of a pillbox?

"Damp matches, sir," I said.

"Damp matches!"

"Yes, sir."

The following week I found myself in charge of the annual audit of the mess silverware, having to count knives, forks, spoons, tankards, soup tureens, and napkin rings. Then I escaped for several days on maneuvers with a field artillery battery, to which I was appointed infantry liaison officer. The artillery unit's officers were a friendly crowd, glad to have me along. During the day I rode around in an open Land-Rover, jouncing over the open grassland that stretched back from the coast. I took part in conferences in camouflaged bivouacs and learned what the artillery meant by targeting and bracketing. One almost airless night I moved out of my tent and slept in the open. The sky was vast but the stars hazy, their sparkle subdued into a cloudy incandescence. I could hear the rumble of surf on the shore and from a nearby fishing village the beat of drums. Perhaps a celebration, with much palm-wine drinking, though the sultry night gave the sound an edge of menace. Toward midnight the drums faded. In the morning at first parade and roll call one of the African artillery troopers was found to be missing. It was thought that he might have gone to the village to gatecrash the shindig. His body was discovered later that day on the beach, apparently rolled in by the surf, with a six-inch nail driven into his head. The civil powers—the police—were at once called in, but from what I heard later they were unable to make an arrest; the trooper had apparently offended against local custom and the local gods.

I had a man-management problem of my own. My batman or boy, Bukare Grunshi, had been one of three members of the platoon who had volunteered for the job; he had been a boy for another officer, since departed for home, and Sergeant Seidu recommended him as the best of the three. As was the case with his fellows, he had signed on for ten years; had done so, like many of the others, because of the difficulties of finding any other way of scratching a living in the drought-dominated Northern Territories; the Gold Coast Regiment offered him a dwelling, a small wage, and two square meals a day thrown in. Bukare had a sharply angled face with a jutting chin; his head was flat-topped, covered with bristly black hair. He was in his mid-twenties. His customary clothing when not on parade was a white singlet and a pair of faded blue football shorts, from which his long legs stuck out, scarred with pink-gray blotches, the result of yaws and malnutrition. On active duty a batman serves as platoon messenger, carrying the platoon commander's orders to each section when necessary; and the danger he is thus exposed to under fire makes up for the comparative comfort of his normal routine, which is free from many platoon duties. If I'd been stationed in England, I would have been expected to share the services of a batman with several other subalterns. Here I alone had Bukare, and in consequence he wasn't overworked.

In the mornings, after bringing in tea and shaving water, he would carry in my boots, shirt, shorts, belt, and parade hat. During the morning while I was working with the platoon Bukare would do odd jobs, put my mess kit in order, clean out my room, and chat with the other boys. They would take turns going to the kitchens to bring back their food. After one-thirty when the heat was intense and the day's work was largely done, Bukare would sit on the veranda outside my gidda, dozing, sometimes combing his hair and staring intently at himself in the small steel mirror that he carried in the back pocket of his shorts. Bukare's vanity, I soon realized, was matched by his ability to cut corners. Sometimes he would judge that a pair of my shorts didn't need washing and starching but could be made presentable with a sponge-down and a press with a hot iron. My boots were never the shiniest on parade at 3 GCR, and I imagined that Smallwood would eventually reprimand me and tell me get a grip on my boy.

Bukare and I had restricted conversations, or "palavers," as they were called. Pidgin English was a constraint, and so was the master-servant relationship; Bukare's problems, insofar as I received word of them, generally had to do with dissatisfaction he and the other boys felt about the quality of the rice they had been given at lunchtime or the fact that I had forgotten to give him money to buy a new can of brass polish or charcoal for his iron. Over and above his ordinary army pay, I gave Bukare a weekly "dash" of ten shillings. He had a wife and child. Unlike some of the other soldiers, who were mission-educated, he had never been to school, and I showed him how to write his name.

I told Bukare about my leave a few weeks in advance. While I was away, I explained, he was to work with the platoon—otherwise he would have nothing to do for the fortnight I was absent. Sergeant Seidu would find out if he could still fire a rifle and dismantle a Bren gun. Bukare appeared to receive this order in his usual phlegmatic manner. He said, "Sir," and continued to stand there. When he saw that I had nothing else to say, he left and went back out to the porch.

In the last few days before I set off, Bukare was busier than I'd ever seen him. Had I maligned him in thinking him indolent? While I was reading or trying to write during the afternoons, he would take from the wardrobe things that he had already washed and pressed, and would remove them to the veranda, from which came the sound of his scrubbing brush and the smell of burning charcoal. One evening, as I set out to walk across to the mess for dinner, I found him staring at his distorted reflection in the chromed fuel tank of the motorcycle, which he had obviously been polishing. He had even washed the tires, which had been coated with thick red dust, and after a few minutes' riding on the laterite roads would be again. That evening he packed my clothes and traveling gear in two rucksacks, to be hung over the rear mudguard. Then he sat for a long time outside my room, as if waiting for further orders.

The next morning I intended to leave after first parade. I hurried through my instructions to Sergeant Seidu; he had a full program of training to carry out while I was away. I reminded him that Bukare Grunshi was to work with the platoon until I returned.

"Yes, sir," said Sergeant Seidu. The creases of a frown appeared on his usually flawless forehead. He looked in the direction of the men's huts behind me.

"Well?" I said.

"I no think Bukare Grunshi agree for that. He tell Lance-Corporal Ankrah he no go for regular duties. He a boy."

I told him what I had already said to Bukare, and that I would repeat it before leaving.

"Yes, sir," the sergeant said doubtfully.

"Sergeant Seidu," I said, trying for what I hoped would sound like iron firmness, "Bukare Grunshi is to train with the platoon. There's nothing else for him to do."

"Yes, sir." Sergeant Seidu swung a sudden brisk salute, which didn't at all succeed in conveying assurance.

As I walked back to my giddah, I wondered whether this was proof of Bukare Grunshi's idleness—clearly he wanted two weeks' holiday now in addition to the regular leave he would get later in the year. Was he testing my will, fairly certain I would end by saying, "All right, Bukare, but just don't make yourself conspicuous while I'm away"? Or was he afraid that if he went back to the platoon I would choose another boy when I returned? Perhaps it was simply my failure to communicate, or his denseness—he hadn't understood the order. Or perhaps there was some mysterious African reason that I would never fathom.

Bukare was sitting on the veranda; his comb and mirror lay beside him. Two other boys were at work outside their officers' rooms. I walked up and put a hand on the saddle of the BSA, already hot from the sun. Bukare stood up, not looking at me. Slowly and quietly I told him again that while I was away he was to rejoin the platoon. I said finally, "Do you understand, Bukare?"

"Sir, I understand. But I your boy, sir."

"Yes. But there will be nothing for you to do. No boots to clean, no brass to polish. You report to Sergeant Seidu for regular duties."

Bukare looked at his feet, which were bare, and shook his head. "I no go for platoon, sir."

"Why not?"

"I your boy. I stay here and look after your kit, sir."

I was aware that the other two boys had ceased chattering to one another and were straining to hear what was going on. I explained to Bukare that if he didn't obey orders he left me no choice. He repeated his protestation that he was a boy and wouldn't join the platoon. I called over one of the other boys and sent him for Sergeant Seidu. Then I went into my room and changed into a civilian shirt, exchanging my boots for shoes. I brought out the rucksacks and strapped them to the motorcycle. Bukare stood there, staring out toward the patch of garden in front of the veranda. I tried to remember the wording of the command to arrest someone. He would probably get ten days. Sergeant Seidu came trotting up, followed by my messenger. The sergeant halted and saluted. I asked him to explain the situation to Bukare Grunshi in his own language, since my English didn't seem effective. The sergeant did so. Bukare did not reply. He looked slowly at me and then at his comb and mirror, which lay in the shade of the veranda. Sergeant Seidu gave me a cautious, almost nervous glance. The two boys stood nearby, shuffling.

"Sergeant," I said, "fall in Bukare Grunshi between these two men. March him to the guard room and put him on a charge. Insubordination."

"Yes, sir."

"Go on then."

"*Sir!*" With an air of relief, Sergeant Seidu turned on Bukare. "Grunshi—fall in!"

Bukare stood to attention between his two colleagues, who looked more worried than he did. His eyes seemed glazed. Sergeant Seidu saluted me again and I returned the salute, forgetting for the moment that I was in civilian clothes. Bukare Grunshi said, "I be boy." Then he was marched away, the sergeant giving the performance a disciplinary air by shouting out the step at the three of them. "Left, right, left, right, left..."

I got onto my motorcycle, gave the starting pedal a fierce kick, and rode off to look for the Tano temple.

# 22

MUCH LATER THIS DIFFICULTY WITH BUKARE—MY "SERvant problem"—came to seem my most tangible encounter with the nature of colonial power, almost an allegory in which I had become involved, a close-at-hand demonstration of failure to perceive and steer and encourage. But not long afterward I decided that what probably had been at the root of Bukare's mulishness was boots. It was a matter that had arisen before. A special extra-wide-toed boot was made for African soldiers, who were descended from people who had been walking barefoot for centuries. But many of the soldiers disliked the look of these boots, and did their best to exchange them for the regular British model, which wasn't exactly pointy-toed. Bukare had made this attempt, and failed; the quartermaster's store did not have a British boot that would contain Bukare's huge splayed-out toes. Bukare had made trouble on a route march, preferring to go barefoot rather than wear the wide-toed boots that fashion—the opinion of his fellows—declared grotesque. Back in the platoon on normal duties he would have to wear the hated boots again.

Although the incident soured the start of my expedition, I had put it to the back of my mind after half an hour's riding. I had written home on first getting this motorcycle, "The BSA responds with a roar to the slightest twist of the throttle"—and now, on the coast road west of Accra, the same euphoria possessed me. The road was about the width of an English country lane, with little traffic apart from a Peugeot painted in Convention People's Party colors, with a loudspeaker on the roof, heading no doubt for a village to blare out CPP exhortations, and the occasional mammy-wagon—the brightly painted, open three-ton trucks used as unscheduled buses. Their owner-drivers usually decorated them with slogans and invocations like "God my Maker, He defend You," and "Be Brave and Fear the Lord," which perhaps gave everyone in them secure feelings as the trucks bounced along, taking up most of the road (there was no white dividing line) until the last moment before reaching an oncoming vehicle, in this case me; and then swerving wildly to give me room, the mammy-wagon passengers all waving and shouting as if this sort of excitement really made their journey. The joys of the road! But as the morning advanced the wagons were fewer, and by noon I seemed to have the road to myself. I stopped at twelve-thirty in the shade of a huge tree and rested the motorbike on its side, since the ground of the verge was too soft to support the stand. I ate a sandwich and studied my map. I took some photographs to record this opening stage of my expedition. When I decided that it was time to get going again, I discovered that the back tire was flat.

Fortunately I had tire irons, a kit for patching the inner tube, and a pump. But it meant removing the rucksacks and taking off the back wheel. I was getting my hands covered with black oil from the chain when a small mammy-wagon drew up and its entire load of passengers got out—eleven young men and boys. The driver was the only one who wore European clothes. And they all pitched in: two or three took over the repair job while the others encouraged them; they fixed the puncture and replaced the wheel and chain. I took their photograph to commemorate the event and gave the leader of the party a small dash. They shouted and waved at me as they drove off.

But I wasn't able to celebrate by driving off just yet. I was wiping my hands on the coarse roadside grass when an army Land-Rover pulled up: African driver, British officer as passenger; the back full of suitcases and boxes. The officer—smartly turned out, a major—asked if I was all right, and I said yes, thank you. He recognized me as someone he had seen on a recent visit to the battalion in Accra. He introduced himself: Major Clarke, on the way from 2 GCR in Takoradi to take command of 3 GCR. I said, "How do you do, sir?" and gave him my name.

"Off for a weekend spin?"

"No, sir. Leave, sir." I gave him a brief synopsis of my plans.

"Ah. So you won't be with us for the Queen's Birthday Parade?"

" 'Fraid not, sir."

"Mmmm."

My new commanding officer drove off, looking as if he had run into his first 3 GCR problem.

Most of the larger settlements in the Gold Coast had rest houses, which provided simple overnight accommodation for travelers. At Saltpond, where I stopped with such a stay in mind, the rest house was locked; the caretaker was away. Luckily the Scottish doctor and his wife who lived next door were hospitable; they gave me dinner as well as a room for the night. The doctor had read a good deal about the history of the coast, and we talked about the lure of gold, the slaves, and the trading companies. The Portuguese, Dutch, and Danish had all in turn been here, but the British bullied their way in and had, until now, persisted. "Good idea to go out and see things for yourself," said the doctor, "but don't imagine that you'll find it easy to get under the surface. This country's developed a thick skin, against mosquitoes, against Europeans." The room his wife showed me to had a view of the moonlit sea. Surf crashed on the rocks of a little bay, unseen below.

The following day was one of forts and castles. In the morning I stopped at a village called Abadiz, which had the remnants of a fort. By ten I was in the town of Cape Coast, standing outside the tall white walls of Cape Coast castle. This had been built in the late seventeenth century as the headquarters of the Royal African Company—there had been a Swedish fort on the site—on a rocky headland against which the Atlantic breakers pounded, filling the air with a fine spray. Inside the walls, I peered down into deep vaults, cut out of the rock, which had been used to house a thousand men and women at a time as they awaited transshipment as slaves to the Americas. The aperture I looked through was small, one of several meant to ventilate the vaults below. A few miles further on was Elmina, an equally imposing fortress, the first European building in the tropics, started by the Portuguese in 1482 (Christopher Columbus is thought to have been on the expedition). The name, in Portuguese, meant "the mine"; it was where the Portuguese acquired gold, brought down from places up-country, by bartering goods brought from Europe. There was a deep moat, which reminded me of Portchester, and along the stone battlements old cannon pointed out to sea and inland.

I knew from what I'd read at Achimota that these forts and castles had been built to withstand attacks from both directions—from other Europeans and from the natives, though there was often a modus vivendi with people in the immediate vicinity. The bastions and ramparts had usually been constructed so that they didn't encroach on ground precious to the adjacent community—sacred or fetish rocks, for instance. Here at Elmina the walls seemed to form a shelter for a score of native surf boats that were pulled up on the beach. The white walls were in need of repair, however, and various relatively modern structures within looked bedraggled. In 1637, Elmina had been captured from the Portuguese by the Dutch, who transferred it to the British in 1872. The British had abolished the slave trade in 1807. Standing on the battlements, looking westward along the coast, thinking of Granddad Molony—who had been here fifty years before, when, as my mother always said, the Gold Coast had been called the white man's grave—thinking of castles and the way they symbolize conquest and make permanent the unease between those who come from abroad and those who are native, watching the surf roll in and a boat with fishermen come shooting through it, I felt no great pangs of guilt from being a young representative of the white race. Pretty soon the locals would be in sole charge of these castles, and have to decide whether to spend money on mortar and whitewash for their walls.

There was no rest house at Elmina. I backtracked to Cape Coast to the rest house there—comfortable quarters including cooking facilities, even a can opener. But during the night I woke in a heavy sweat. My stomach was being pulled in different directions, with sharp pains. A few months before I'd had strange spasms within, diagnosed as the effect on a stomach muscle of too much curry, and treated with daily doses of belladonna. This was something else, possibly early intimations of the white man's grave. I stayed in the bathroom most of the night—in fact, quite often in the bath, submersed in cold water and then hot water, whichever seemed right to deal with fever or a feeling of being frozen. It was at least as bad as being seasick, and as with seasickness it continued even when the sickness lacked a wherewithal. In the morning the caretaker found me some aspirins. I drank pints of water. It was, I imagined, some sort of dysentery—I hoped not the sort that lasted on and off for a year. At midday, shivering and shaking, I climbed onto the BSA and headed for Takoradi—my destination 2 GCR and the battalion medical officer. I rode slowly, concentrating on the road as well as I could, the countryside a blur.

I spent four days in Takoradi, taking the huge white sulfa-guanadine pills the M.O. dispensed to me, in bed most of the time, listening to the battalion band playing during the Queen's birthday parade. I didn't appear much in the mess, and the 2 GCR officers didn't have a chance to inquire at length into what had brought me here. My feelings of wretched disappointment—my expedition blasted—were slightly assuaged by rain, which fell throughout two of the days and would have made any movement difficult. Then, still feeling weak and looking pallid under my tan, I thought, Well, now or never, and set off inland, on the main road to Kumasi, one hundred and thirty miles away. Along it, as I had marked on my map, was the place where I had to turn west for the source of the Tano. I had just about the strength to grip the handlebars. Great trees overhung the laterite road as it passed through the rain forest. In the centers of villages there were shrines and altars to local deities. I reached the junction with the road to the west, and turned along it. The road seemed to diminish, or the forest to thicken. "I'll just see how it goes for a little while," I thought, and almost immediately had to stop. Doubled with cramp, I put my head on the handlebars; perhaps I passed out briefly. When I sat up again, it was to notice a man standing twenty yards or so away among the trees, watching me. He was an old dark brown man and very tall—very old and immensely powerful. He was quite silent and motionless, wearing a fine cloth and carrying what looked like an intricately carved stick. I pointed weakly ahead along the road and said, "Tano?" He still didn't speak or even nod, though I thought I detected what might have been a smile. Then another cramp seized me, and I had to put my head down. When I looked up the old man was no longer there.

In Kumasi I took shelter with the army again, and the mess of the Gold Coast Regiment's Training Centre, where recruits were put through their first paces, provided cheap room and board for the last week of my leave—which was also a convalescence. The rain fell; it was, after all, the rainy season, and Kumasi was in the rain belt. Rain in great drops bounced off the tin roof of the giddah I'd been given and poured down the window like liquid film, through which the dark green of the surrounding vegetation was apparent like submarine growth. The grass of the lawns around the mess was coarse but vivid compared to the bleached stuff we had in Accra. At night I needed a blanket on my bed, and it was a pleasure to slide under it and feel again the contrast between chill night air and bed warmth. I read *Punch* in the mess lounge and flirted with the quartermaster's daughter, Dorothy, who was seventeen and pretty and not too blasé as a result of all the attention she received. The BSA was now misfunctioning—the timing, so I was told, by a local expert who thought he had put it right—and since I was still feeling fragile I took the train back to Accra, with the motorcycle in the guard's van.

# 23

BAD TIMING LANDED ME ALMOST AT ONCE IN TROUBLE during my first week back on duty at Teshie. The motorcycle broke down on the road back from Accra on Thursday afternoon; it was too hot and too far to push it home. Major Watson, the acting commanding officer, striving to impress the authorities with his competence, had declared Thursdays a "transportless day," which meant that training-school vehicles were to be used only for emergencies and journeys of the highest military priority. Did I forget this diktat or conveniently push it to the back of my mind? I knew that if I left the BSA by the roadside for more than an hour it would disappear—perhaps abruptly, in one piece; perhaps stripped down item by item, as by piranhas. I hitched a ride to Teshie, ran to the motor transport office, told the African sergeant that I was borrowing a one-tonner and driver for half an hour, and drove out to pick up the BSA. The driver and I loaded it on the truck. As we were coming back into the gates of the training school I glimpsed a florid mustache. Major Watson walked across the roadway between the mess and his office. The phone was ringing on the M.T. Sergeant's desk when I got there.

Was it a court-martial offense? That week concluded my appointed tour of duty at Teshie, and Major Watson, bidding me a curt farewell, told me that he had handed on the disposition of the matter to Major Clarke at 3 GCR, and that Major Clarke, as my commanding officer, would decide whether to refer it to the Brigadier.

As it turned out, a few days after my return to the battalion, Smallwood summoned me. The suspense was heightened momentarily when his first pithy remarks contained a few hints of compliment—he didn't want to sully my fairly positive military record. I had proved myself *for the most part* a reasonably useful young officer. However. Orders were orders. Discipline was discipline. My punishment was seven days' duty as orderly officer.

Bukare Grunshi had resumed his batman tasks for me; he apparently bore me no grudge for his ten days' sentence; and he now rose to the occasion. So did my fellow subalterns. It was onerous enough being orderly officer for the day, inspecting the guards at military premises in various parts of Accra at different times of day and night—but a week! Bukare kept my boots and leather Sam Browne belt splendidly polished. And my friends took turns at spelling me at some of the nocturnal duties as the week proceeded. (I was, through my transgression and penance, saving them from taking their regular day's turn at the job.) For the first time I found myself bathed in the quasi-romantic, pseudo-heroic glow of the gallant miscreant. My friend Peter Hooker said, with an air of experience in these things, "I shouldn't worry, Tony. They'll have marked you down quietly as someone who shows initiative." Curiously, a part of me did care what the army thought of me. With my Teshie colleagues Nigel McKeand and John Heritage, I'd discussed the compulsory part-time service we were going to do while at university, and John and I had decided that we were going to volunteer for the Special Air Services, the outfit which in later years became Britain's chief weapon against foreign terrorists, but about which then we knew mostly that service with it involved learning to ski, parachute, and train for combat in small groups in difficult terrain. To Nigel this desire seemed altogether too gung-ho.

Another worry was whether the army was going to let me out in time to start at Merton in October. West Africa Command affected uncertainty about a concession allowing university entrants to serve only twenty-one months; there were rumors that the list of National Servicemen waiting to fly back to England was long and that the planes were running behind schedule. But the closer the date came, on which I ought to leave, the less it bothered me. In many ways I was unready to leave Africa. There was still so much to be done. I had a feeling—felt in other circumstances since—of bouncing against a wall that kept me from a world of absolute fascination on the other side; there were doors through it, ways over it or under it, if one had the patience and wit to seek them out, but I hadn't found them yet. It was frustrating. I suspected that the process of getting through to the other side had to do with myself and who I was—and that, too, was uncertain. But I took what opportunities came up in the remaining weeks. Smallwood helped. Whether as a supplementary punishment—knowing my week's duty had been made easier for me by my pals—or because he realized I had an interest in the country and might as well be indulged in it ("Halfway to going bush, if you ask me, but he won't be here long," I imagined him saying), he detailed me to go to Kumasi again, this time to collect for the battalion a draft of recruits who had just completed their basic training.

I caught the train. First-class rail travel was an officer's privilege in England, too, but on Gold Coast Railways first-class was extra special, each compartment having only four seats—armchairs, really—two on each side divided by little tables. Overhead a fan revolved. On the northern edge of the coastal plain the railway passed into the more fertile countryside where cocoa was grown: field after field of small trees. The cocoa beans that grew on these provided much of the wealth of the country. The train stopped now and then at villages, and at one small station three people entered the compartment, which I had had to myself until then. A family, I assumed—man, wife, daughter; well-to-do, judging from the fine cloths they wore. Perhaps the man was a cocoa farmer. He exchanged nods of greeting with me and sat down in the chair on my side. His wife sat across from him and the girl, in the other window seat, opposite me. She was, I guessed, about seventeen, demurely pretty, with close-cropped hair, and her cloth or lappa reaching to her ankles, her feet in simple sandals stretched out on the floor a few inches from my brown shoes. I looked out through the window, seeing both the passing landscape and the muzzy reflection of the compartment in the glass. Cutting across this double exposure I felt I ought to be able to add the girl's appraisal of me, a quid pro quo for mine of her; but this didn't seem to come. After a few words to his wife the man closed his eyes; in a little while she dozed, too.

The English humorist Stephen Potter has provided several opening gambits for a young man who wants to address a young woman in a train compartment—one is, as she opens a newspaper, "Ah, I see *The Times* is being published again." (Part of the humor of that remark resides in the fact that when he made this joke, which was several years after my African sojourn, *The Times* had never missed an issue.) No equivalent remark, suited to the circumstances, came to me. I assumed she would know some English but I wasn't sure. I looked at the floor—at two ranks of pink-brown toes, the big toe on each foot pressed slightly apart by a dividing thong. As if of its own accord, my left foot moved a mere inch toward her left foot, which was the closer. I looked at the small, shrublike cocoa trees, at a far hill that rose in an abrupt dome above a line of hills. The fan turned. I thought I could hear her parents breathe. I glanced at the floor. Her left foot had moved an inch or so closer to mine. The next move was up to me, and I shut my eyes, wondering if I had the nerve to do it. What if her move had been accidental? What if she complained? And then with a twitch that seemed once again to place the responsibility on my foot rather than on me, I slid the outside edge of my left foot alongside hers. For an instant I thought, It will move away. But it didn't—it stayed there for a moment, and then slowly it moved round inside my left foot, so that it was hidden behind it, pressed between my left foot and right foot.

Her eyes were closed—as I saw when I took the quickest of glimpses. I could hear my heart beating. I wondered whether her father would wield a machete if he woke and saw. Our pretense, of course, was that we were both asleep, had no idea what was going on, were unaware that our feet were interwoven, pressed together. I could feel the warmth and pulsation of her through my shoes—damn my shoes! The barest tremors passed back and forth between us. I looked out at the cocoa farms. Villages. Hills. I listened to the clatter of the train wheels and whir of the fan, and I felt the rhythmic rocking of the carriage and the circling waves of warm air. The idyll lasted for I don't know how long, and then suddenly, with no warning, it was over; her foot was withdrawn. A second later her father said something to her mother, who looked into a bag. They gave the appearance of collecting themselves, and then, as the train began to slow down for a station, they rose—the man went out into the corridor first, followed by his wife, followed by the girl. I watched them walk past along the laterite platform, the girl not giving even a hint of a glance at the window of my compartment, little clouds of dust rising around her ankles.

A week later I rode the BSA up into that country. The motorcycle's timing was fixed, and it was going well again. I had made a deal with a newly arrived officer who was going to buy it when I left. I was enjoying my last excursions on it. I went looking for the hill that I had seen from the train and which jutted up above the rest of the range; in my reading, I had seen it mentioned as a sacred hill. It was over toward the Volta, the other great river of the country, and it took me several hours to get there on narrow tracks. I stopped in a village near the base. I didn't want to intrude—I remembered the man with the spike through his head. But when some children and then an elderly man approached and seemed ready to talk, I pointed to the hill and asked him if I could climb it. The old man nodded—he would come with me, I gathered. A woman in a nearby hut was appointed guardian of the motorcycle. The old man disappeared for a minute and came back carrying a rusty Tate & Lyle Golden Syrup tin. I brought my rucksack, which had some lunch in it. Then he set off ahead of me. It was a scrubby, rocky ascent, the path furrowed into a trench by rain. A sort of cactus grew on the rough ground. At the top, there was a circle of stones and a view to all points of the compass—though I couldn't see the Accra-Kumasi railway line. My guide muttered a few words and poured a fluid—it looked dark and red—from the Golden Syrup tin into a pot, which sat in a hole in the center of the ring of stones. He stood aside. I felt a compulsion—as much social or amicable as religious, perhaps—to do something similar. In my water bottle I had some Rose's Lime Juice diluted with water, and I proffered this. The old man agreed. I poured my libation—a liberal cupful—into the pot. On the way down the hill, I wondered if it was imagination that made the old man seem very much like the elderly man I had seen, or thought I had seen, when gripped with dysentery pains on the track toward the Tano.

Had my fellow subalterns known, they would have said that I was indeed showing all the signs. The week before, a British sergeant had been discovered at 3 GCR dressed in an African cloth, going into the soldiers' lines to drink palm wine and join them in the gods knew what else. A short-service lieutenant had recently had what was called a nervous breakdown and had been shipped back to England. As he was loaded into the plane, he was reported to have shouted "Africa! Africa!" as he might have cried the name of a lost loved one. A year was perhaps as long as one could stand, and for me it was coming up to that. Or was it something to do with the need to belong, wherever one was? It might in any event soon be the Gordon's gin in the surf. Soon, obsessed with the toes and ankles of the farmer's daughter, I might be found prowling among the cocoa plantations.

On my last Sunday I rode eastward along the coast, toward Tema, a fishing town where it was planned to build a new deep-sea port. I turned off along a track across the savanna of rough grass and scattered, spindly trees, until I reached the dunes. It was a lonely spot—no sign of a settlement or of people. The beach was absolutely empty. Looking each way I could see only the surf rolling in and, in the air above, the shimmering haze of spray that formed a sort of translucent, transcendent surf. The rollers were not so high as at Labadi, and I swam in them for a while. Then I sat on the sand, close to the water's edge, where it was dark and slightly damp. Reaching out, my hands scooped up some sand and kneaded it into a mound; with a depression in the top, this became a bowl or basin. Next I made a range of hills, with one higher dome-shaped hill. I moved up on the beach to drier, warmed sand. I formed it into a larger shape, almost my length—head, arms, torso, breasts, pelvis, thighs, calves, ankles. The sand was getting hot as I finished molding it—the cocoa farmer's daughter—mother earth, now crumbling—Africa!

# 24

AT THE THIRTY-TWO YEARS' DISTANCE FROM WHICH I write, my return to England from Africa seems like a natural conclusion to an epoch in my life. It was also an echo of my first coming back, setting up reverberations that would travel onward and coalesce into a pattern containing future returns. But at the time the sense of a period coming to a close coexisted with the blurring onrush of the present, and the somewhat stomach-hollowing expectations of what might be about to happen. The plane that took me back was again a Viking, flying on more or less the same route on which I'd come out. The sky began to darken as the plane crossed the Channel. Small white flecks on gray, seen below, were perhaps what then made me remember the *Ranee,* and the end of that earlier voyage home. Both exiles had been involuntary; both had brought about a desire for involvement in the place in which I willy-nilly found myself. Now the coastline appeared, the mass of the land darker than the sea—a coastline suddenly recognizable as that of Hampshire. I could see Poole, just in Dorset, off to the left, and the western Solent and Lymington River below. The port wing, like the shutter of time, passed over them. I remembered the islands with creeks, estuaries, bays, and hills I'd drawn as a boy, and the shape of the island of which England was a part formed in my mind, with all its bumps, dents, bulges, and creases, a worn and burdened scrap of the world's surface bounded by the sea. The plane turned east a little. Lights were appearing down below, along roads, and from crescents and squares of houses. Park Gate. Swanwick. Fareham. Portchester. I was flying over my own childhood. It hadn't been long ago—this was where, as much as anywhere, I belonged—and yet I felt for the moment a strange detachment, reminding me of that time when, awake or dreaming, I had imagined that I was floating over my own body and had a surprising independence from it, could go anywhere without it. And yet there had also been a touch of fear that I would not be able to rejoin it, to get back into it as I ultimately needed to.

The two engines changed their note as the pilot throttled them back and the Viking began to make a bumpy descent toward Blackbushe. Although we were not yet near the ground, I clutched the arms of the seat to be ready for any shocks of landing.